KILTS AND KISSES AT HIGHLAND HALL

HANNAH LYNN

B
Boldwood

First published in Great Britain in 2025 by Boldwood Books Ltd.

Copyright © Hannah Lynn, 2025

Cover Design by Alexandra Allden

Cover Images: Shutterstock

A CIP catalogue record for this book is available from the British Library.

Paperback ISBN 978-1-83603-841-2

Large Print ISBN 978-1-83603-842-9

Hardback ISBN 978-1-83603-840-5

Ebook ISBN 978-1-83603-843-6

Kindle ISBN 978-1-83603-844-3

Audio CD ISBN 978-1-83603-835-1

MP3 CD ISBN 978-1-83603-836-8

Digital audio download ISBN 978-1-83603-838-2

This book is printed on certified sustainable paper. Boldwood Books is dedicated to putting sustainability at the heart of our business. For more information please visit https://www.boldwoodbooks.com/about-us/sustainability/

Boldwood Books Ltd, 23 Bowerdean Street, London, SW6 3TN

www.boldwoodbooks.com

ALSO BY HANNAH LYNN

The Holly Berry Sweet Shop Series

The Sweet Shop of Second Chances

Love Blooms at the Second Chances Sweet Shop

High Hopes at the Second Chances Sweet Shop

Family Ties at the Second Chances Sweet Shop

Sunny Days at the Second Chances Sweet Shop

A Summer Wedding at the Second Chances Sweet Shop

Snowflakes Over the Second Chances Sweet Shop

Happy Ever After at the Second Chances Sweet Shop

The Wildflower Lock Series

New Beginnings at Wildflower Lock

Coffee and Cake at Wildflower Lock

Blue Skies Over Wildflower Lock

Forever Love at Wildflower Lock

The Highland Hall Series

Kilts and Kisses at Highland Hall

Standalone Novels

In at the Deep End

The Side Hustle

Hannah Lynn writing as H. M. Lynn

The Head Teacher The Student

The Valentine's Date

To Edwin, Steve and all those we wish were still beside us

1

Nigel clicked the end of his pen. On, then off. On, then off. On and off. If he did it one more time, Bex was going to grab it from his hand and throw it out of their seventh-floor office window. Or at least, that was what she would have liked to do. She wouldn't do that, because Nigel was her boss, and despite her being the most valuable person on the accounting team – his words, not hers – she suspected he wouldn't take too kindly to it.

Still, that incessant clicking noise was making her nervous, and there was no need for her to be nervous, was there? Of course not. The firm was expanding, not downsizing, and even if it had been, she would be nowhere near the top of the redundancy list. So why had Nigel called her into his office with such formality this morning, and why was he having such a hard time spitting his words out? In her heart, she knew there could only be one reason. A very, very positive one.

As she waited for him to put the pen down, or at least stop clicking it long enough to say something to her, she regretted her decision to take a seat. Her knee was bouncing up and down as she tried to act calm and composed. Nonchalant, even. Like she hadn't seen this day coming for years. Like she hadn't been working her butt off for this promotion since she first took the job here. There would be bubbles with the girls tonight, that was for sure. Screw the fact it was a Monday. She was going to be an associate director. As soon as Nigel found his damn voice.

Finally, with a sharp breath in, Nigel gave the pen one last click before placing it down on the desk in front of him.

'I want you to know that what I'm about to ask of you is a great compliment,' he said.

As butterflies swarmed in Bex's stomach, she tried to keep her expression neutral. Like she hadn't been expecting this. For ten years, she'd been working at the same accountancy firm, and she had done more than her fair share of grunt work. As a manager, she had been given the most difficult team to lead and the most difficult clients to handle. She had attended every workplace bonding retreat and voluntary staff training the firm had offered and sacrificed more hours than anyone could have dreamt, and it had all been leading up to this point. Associate director. That was the role Nigel was about to tell her she had got. The role she deserved.

'I want you to know that I won't let you down,' she replied, trying to suppress the grin rising on her lips.

'I know, Rebecca. I can assure you that I thought very hard about the right person for this position, and what it came down to was that I needed someone I could trust. I needed someone completely professional, who always puts the job first. Who can work under pressure and in difficult situations, and I mean this truthfully when I say there was only one person I knew would fit that bill.' He paused and smiled slightly. 'And you're that person,' he added, as if she hadn't got that bit.

'Thank you, Nigel. That means a lot to me.'

Again, a silence filled the air. Bex's heart was pounding so forcefully she could feel the blood rushing behind her ears. Why wouldn't he just say it? He wanted her to be the new associate director. It really wasn't that hard to say, was it?

She cleared her throat, wondering if perhaps she should say something more. Like how she was sure they would make a great team and how the vision of the firm would always be at the forefront of what she did. Yet as she opened her mouth to speak, Nigel picked up the pen, clicked it once more, and looked at her with an almost apologetic expression on his face.

'I need you to go to Scotland,' he said.

'Sorry?' she said, sure she must have misheard him.

'Scotland,' he repeated. 'I need you to go to Scotland. For two months.'

2

'You have to be joking? Scotland, for two months? Why?'

Bex had gone straight from the office to Wildflower Lock to visit her friend Daisy on her narrowboat. She'd sent a single message before she left: 'Have drink ready.' And Daisy had clearly taken note as a variety of wines were now open on the table in front of them. Bex had also called their other friend, Claire, to say that she was needed too, and now the three of them were sitting together on the boat, jaws hanging loose as Bex relayed the meeting to them.

'I mean, the good thing is, if I do this, then apparently I can choose whatever jobs I want from now on. And I assume that means the associate director role.'

'But why do you have to go?' Claire said. 'Surely you would have to apply for a job like this. You can't just be sent there.'

Bex pursed her lips. This wasn't like in the office with Nigel, where she had to bite her tongue and appear appreciative and say she was grateful for the opportunity. She was here with her friends. She could tell them the truth.

'I'm single,' she said with a shrug. 'Meaning, from the firm's point of view, I don't have anyone who'll miss me when I'm up there for two months.'

The anger that flashed across her friends' faces was the exact confirmation she had needed that it was okay to be furious at the situation.

'What? That is not true!'

'Did he say that? That's discrimination.'

She was grateful for how riled her friends had become on her behalf. Unfortunately, it didn't change the situation.

'Of course, he didn't say it like that,' Bex said. 'He used the word "committed" a lot. Other people had personal commitments... family commitments. I don't. God, there's nothing like being reminded how painfully single you are than being sent hundreds of miles away because no one will miss you.'

'We'll miss you!' Daisy and Claire spoke in unison, and for the first time since she'd received the news, Bex felt a flutter of warmth fill her. She smiled weakly.

'I know, but it's not quite the same.'

'And what about your flat? You have a home here.'

'I know, but apparently there's enough accommodation at this place that I won't need to pay rent, so I won't lose out financially. It's just frustrating, you know.' She let out a long groan. 'I'm not wrong to be annoyed by this, am I?' she said, trying to keep the focus on her initial grievances rather than being sidetracked by the reminder of her perpetually single relationship status, but it was difficult given how intertwined the two were. 'I get that I can't keep a relationship going for more than two months, but that doesn't mean I don't have a life. I don't want to just pack everything up and move there. But I can't complain about it, because generally speaking, Nigel's great, and I actually think he believes he's doing me a favour by giving me this position. Besides, he's right. I am the one without "commitments".'

A deep aching sat heavily in her chest. She'd always thought that playing the field was a sensible thing to do, that waiting until Mr Perfect finally showed up would be the key to having the perfect ever-after marriage like her parents had. But her last four relationships had lasted less than three months each, and here she was, over a year older, feeling no closer to finding that happily ever after.

'You just need to think of it as an adventure,' Daisy said, bringing Bex out of her thoughts. 'There are some beautiful areas up in Scotland. All the islands and things. And you won't be working all the time, will you? You'll have time to get out and explore.'

'You haven't actually told us what you're needed to do up there,' Claire said before Bex could respond. 'Why do you need to be up there?'

'It's some friend of Nigel's dad,' she said, though the thought alone was enough to worry her. Nigel was in his late fifties, so she could only imagine what this man was like. 'Apparently, he's got a large estate, with land and various businesses and things, but he hasn't done a great job of keeping on top of all his accounts. It sounds like he's still stuck in the days of paper and wants someone to go up there and sort it all out. Digitalise it, that kind of thing. It's more bookkeeping than accounting. Not my area of expertise at all.' Well, it was beneath her area of expertise – that was what she actually wanted to say, but she kept that to herself, just like she had done in the meeting with Nigel. 'That's all I know. I mean, I'm hoping it'll take less time than Nigel thinks, but I won't know until I get there. And I got the feeling that Nigel expects me to stay up there the full two months, or longer than that if that's how long it takes. If I want the promotion, that is.'

Silence fell among the girls, and Bex reached for her drink, only to find the glass was empty. She'd googled the place Nigel was sending her, and it seemed to be a little village in the middle of nowhere. The chances of them having a decent wine shop felt next to nothing. She would need to stock up.

'You never know,' Daisy said. 'Maybe you'll find your Scottish Prince Charming up there? I have always liked a man in a kilt.'

Bex arched an eyebrow. 'Let's make one thing clear. I have zero need for a prince, and my one aim is to get the job over and done with as quickly as possible. But I'll be sure to let Theo know about the kilt thing when he gets back.'

As the girls chuckled, Bex's mind drifted back to thoughts of the next two months.

Maybe Daisy was right. Maybe she could turn this into an adventure. And what was the worst-case scenario? If she hated the place, then she could lose herself in the work, get it sorted as quickly as possible, then come back to London to the promotion she'd been working her butt off for, and her friends would still be waiting for her.

She would do this. She would go to Scotland and do what had been asked of her. After all, it wasn't like she had a choice.

3

'How long have you got left to go?' Claire said, her voice tiny through the car's speaker system. 'You must be nearly there now?'

'Three hours,' Bex replied with a groan. 'Remind me again why I decided to drive rather than fly.'

She already knew the answer, of course. If she was going to be in the middle of nowhere, away from tubes and taxis, not to mention everything she loved about London life, then she needed her car to get around. Unfortunately, that meant an eleven-hour drive. She had done half of it the day before and had planned on getting up early to finish off the remaining five hours, but then she had overslept, there had been roadworks and diversions, and for the first three hours of the journey, the time on her satnav kept going up rather than down.

Now it was already gone three in the afternoon, but at least she had passed Glasgow and was on the narrow country lanes, finally feeling like she was making decent progress. Besides, the long summer evenings meant there were still hours of daylight ahead of her.

'I've been researching the village where this house is.' Daisy's voice took over on the phone. 'It looks lovely. Very posh. They hold clay pigeon shoots and country balls, that type of thing.'

'Well, I'm sure that's lovely for the people who live there. I, however, will not have time to do anything other than pretend I'm a bookkeeper for the next two months. Honestly, the more I think about it, the madder I get. But at least it's pretty. Very pretty.'

Pretty was probably the biggest understatement for what she was seeing. It was stunning. Breathtaking even. Whichever window she looked out of, all she could see was miles and miles of constantly changing greenery stretching out in every direction. One moment she was driving through undulating hills; the next, it was long, tundra-like plains, and only a couple of miles later, the green had been replaced entirely by the sight of the sea, pale blue and glinting with sunlight off in the distance.

'That's not the only thing,' Daisy continued. 'The place you're staying at, you said it was called Highland Hall, right?'

'That's right, why?'

'Well, I looked that up too and—'

'What the hell!' Bex slammed on the brakes. Her pulse soared as the car skidded on the stony road and came to a stop only half a foot away from disaster.

'Bex? Is everything okay?'

'Has something happened?'

Even though Bex could hear the worry in her friends' voices, she couldn't reply straight away. Her pulse was still sky high, and she needed to catch her breath. Slowly, she loosened her grip on the steering wheel and managed to choke out an answer.

'Sheep,' she said. 'Lots and lots of sheep.'

* * *

Never before had Bex known sheep to put her in such a foul mood. Normally the only times she saw them were out of the windows of trains or in the fields around Wildflower Lock, and she loved to watch the little bouncing lambs leaping around without a care in the world. But these sheep weren't in a field. They were on the road, and rather than leaping, they were trudging forwards as if they were completely oblivious to the fact that this was a road with traffic on and people in cars who needed to be somewhere.

After apologising to the girls for scaring them, then opening up the camera so they could see what she was having to face, Bex hung up the phone and got out of the car in search of any sign of a farmer or someone she could yell at. But if there was someone there she couldn't see them. So she returned to her vehicle, flicked her audiobook on and tried not to get any more wound up at the massive inconvenience. Finally, after nearly forty minutes, the sheep filtered off the road and into one of the fields.

'Okay, time to make up some of that lost time,' Bex said, pushing her foot down on the accelerator. After her flat, her car was her biggest purchase, and she had spent even longer choosing it. She had wanted something sporty and sleek, but which also had enough space to take all the girls, including Claire's daughter, away for weekends. And so she had finally picked a four-door coupé that ticked all those boxes. Unfortunately, as she weaved down a gently sloping hill and saw a sign at the side of the road, she realised there was one criterion that she definitely hadn't considered when choosing a car.

'Someone somewhere is having a very big laugh at my expense,' she said as she cut the engine, climbed out of the car and walked a little way down the road. Her stomach plummeted at the sight in front of her.

Of course, Bex had heard of fords before. She was an intelligent woman. She had probably driven through one or two of them with her parents when they had gone on holiday to the Cotswolds, but she had never driven through one herself and certainly not in her own car. Her own, expensive, low-to-the-ground car.

She looked at the body of water in front of her. It was slow flowing, but definitely flowing. A river, not a puddle, and probably around ten feet wide. Though it didn't matter how wide it was; what mattered was how deep it was, and that wasn't something she could tell.

'Marvellous, just bloody marvellous,' she said as she turned around, shaking her head. Back in the car, she checked the satnav to see if there were any other routes, and when one appeared, her chest lightened with relief until she noticed that it added another two hours to the journey. *Two hours.* And what if there was another ford on that route, too? She would find herself in exactly the same position. But then, if she flooded the car, she would be in even more trouble. What she needed was some way to work out exactly how deep the water was without risking the car. Which meant there was only one thing she could do.

4

'You are going to pay for this, Nigel.'

Bex was talking to herself through gritted teeth, partially because of how angry she was, but mostly because the water was bloody freezing.

She had rolled up her jeans, grabbed a towel from her bag and walked over to the edge of the ford, at which point she had removed her shoes. She'd initially planned on only going halfway, reasoning that would give her the best indication of how deep it got, but then she also figured there could be some hidden pothole near the other side. It would be a far wiser approach to go all the way across on one side, then back on the other, hopefully gauging where the wheels would drive.

It may have been summer, but the water didn't seem to know that, and every step was painfully cold. Still, she made it to the far side unscathed, before turning around and heading back. By the time she was at her car, drying off her feet, her entire body was covered in goosebumps – even though she had only got wet up to mid-calf. Which meant, thankfully, that the ford was shallow enough for the car to get through.

Even though she knew there should be no issues driving through the shallow water, it didn't stop Bex from holding her breath the entire time. One way or another, she was going to find a way of billing this journey as extra expenses beyond the petrol. Never could she remember having a drive that had left her so fraught. And so much for thinking she was going to pop out for weekends and visit local places. If this was what it was like trying to get to Highland Hall, then she would stay there until the job was done.

Her details from Nigel had told her that Highland Hall was on the outskirts of a village called LochDarroch, about which Bex had done zero research. That wasn't her normal style of things. Normally she liked to do as much research on one of her clients as she could, but normally, she wasn't thrust into living with them, and she had enough to deal with, packing up and coming here, to bother scouting out all the tourist traps. She was a city girl through and through, and as such, LochDarroch, was not somewhere she could imagine liking. Still, as she drove past the little sign, with 'LochDarroch' written on the side, she couldn't help but feel a flutter of guilt for already disliking a place she had never even been. Especially a place that was so unequivocally beautiful.

It could have had something to do with the way the sunlight was glinting off the white painted houses, or the contrast between the dark slate tiles and the pale sky. Or maybe it was the mix of stones that the buildings were made of which combined so perfectly with the rugged landscape and lush green grasses, but whatever the reason, as Bex drove slowly through the village, she found herself drinking it all in. The place that was to be her home for the next two months.

Relief billowed through her as she noticed two pubs, at least one café, and a restaurant too – although only one small shop.

The chances of getting a supermarket delivery here seemed unlikely, but she could cope with eating out. She'd bill it to the firm anyway – after this journey, that was the least she deserved.

As she followed the directions on her satnav, she moved away from the village, passing through a stone lodge gate and onto a gravel driveway.

In her mind, she had created a very loose image of Highland Hall. Given that the village was called LochDarroch, it felt likely that the house would have a view out over the water, and if it had room for her to stay there, it was probably fairly sizeable, but beyond that, she wasn't sure what else to expect. As strange as it might have sounded to Daisy or Claire, she hadn't wanted to look it up. She had been feeling bad enough about having to do this move as it was. The last thing she needed was to see the grey and sombre building she was going to be trapped in for the next eight weeks.

Yet, as the driveway continued, with thick cedar trees marking either side of the route, her nervousness flickered up a notch. This wasn't the driveway of an average house. Or even a larger-than-average house. In fact, she had visited stately homes that had smaller driveways than this. But maybe it was just a Scottish thing. Maybe having all this land meant people liked to spread out more. That was what Bex was thinking when the trees finally gave way to a wide-open driveway. The moment she looked up, one of her hands flew up to her mouth and the nerves in her stomach gave way to a full-on somersault.

'It's a castle,' she said, struggling to take in the building in front of her. 'It's an actual castle.'

5

The car crawled so slowly forward it was barely moving, but Bex didn't want to go any faster; she wanted to take it all in. It was difficult to tell exactly how many turrets the castle had. Maybe four or five, but it also had a moat, round walls, and a wooden door so large you could have fit an elephant through it. But as phenomenal as the building was, so were the grounds. From the angle Bex was sitting at, she couldn't see any sign of the water, but trees and flowers of all shapes, sizes and colours filled the landscape.

Bex had never really been into her flora and fauna growing up, though over recent years, she had spent a substantial amount of time at Wildflower Lock, and Daisy's enthusiasm for all the blooms that grew around her had started to spread. As soon as she got out of the car, she'd need to get photos of these, she thought, and send them to Daisy. Though no sooner had the thought formed than her eyes scrunched closed, and she let out a long yawn.

Why was driving so damn tiring? She had overslept that morning, because the five hours on the road yesterday had taken it out of her. Today was even longer. What she needed was to get a very early night. But before she could do that, she would need to find someone called Fergus. Nigel had told her that Fergus would be her go-to for everything at Highland Hall, though he hadn't actually explained to Bex what his job was. A grounds-man? Another accountant? In a castle like this, he could well be the butler. As soon as she had got her things, she would hunt him down.

There was only one car in front of the house. A large forest-green Land Rover, covered in mud. There had to be another place to park, Bex thought as she drew her car up next to it. After all, a place this size had to be home to a blooming big family, and then there were the staff you'd need to look after everything. She would find where the rest of them parked tomorrow. For now, she just wanted to get in, find this Fergus and get to bed.

Deciding to leave her large suitcase where it was, she got out of the car. Bex had been to Edinburgh before, and given that the trip had been in August, she'd packed for summer weather back then – strappy dresses, denim shorts, flip-flops and sandals. That type of thing. What she'd faced was biting, ferocious winds and a complete lack of any suitable outfits. She hadn't made that mistake this time. Although all she carried with her now was a small bag with a clean change of clothes, pyjamas, washbag and her computer.

She approached the door, fist raised, ready to knock – yet before she could move her hand, a thundering sound caused her to turn her head. Her stomach flipped at the sight.

Five dogs were racing towards her, sprinting with such speed it was like they were a pack about to attack. She turned around, searching for some way to escape them, but there was nowhere to go. And there was no mistaking it now. They were heading straight for her. Did they think she had trespassed on their land? Were they guard dogs trained to attack any intruder? If that was the case, what were they going to do to her?

'Don't let them know you're afraid,' she whispered to herself. 'They mustn't know you're afraid.'

She had heard that dogs sensed fear, but telling herself not to be scared and actually not being scared were very different things. She squeezed her eyes shut, bracing against the pain she was sure was about to strike. But when a sensation finally reached her, it wasn't teeth at all, but a wet, slobbering tongue.

She opened her eyes, only to be knocked back as one of the largest dogs jumped up at her, licking her chin. In seconds, she was surrounded by wagging tails and slobbering jaws.

With relief flooding through her, she straightened up and finally saw behind the wall of dogs, to the old man walking towards her. He was dressed to camouflage perfectly into the scenery – a wax jacket, green flat cap and wooden walking stick.

'Hello,' she said, waving her hand at him. Although whether he didn't see or simply didn't care, she didn't know. He made no attempt to respond, other than by continuing to walk towards her.

His bedraggled hair was sticking out at odd angles beneath his flat cap, and his face wore the beard of a man who had simply lost any desire to shave. The laces of his boots were frayed and untied, and while she suspected it was a green wax jacket he was wearing, it was difficult to tell under the layers of mud. This was not the type of man who had decided to grow old with grace.

The groundskeeper, possibly? she thought. Or perhaps some local homeless man who had come to the castle looking for handouts? Although, his dogs looked remarkably healthy and well. Groundskeeper, then, most likely. She had seen enough period television programmes to know how wealthy families would keep on old and often incapable workers just because they felt guilty about letting them go. That was obviously the case here.

Bex stood up straight. Having given her a terrifying welcome, most of the dogs had disappeared, but one, a red Labrador, had sat down at her side and was continuing to beat its tail on the ground.

'Sorry,' she said, 'I'm Bex – Rebecca Barker. I've been told I need to find Fergus?'

'Aye, I know who you are. Been expecting you.'

The man walked up to the large door, turned the handle and pushed it open. Bex raised an eyebrow. She'd never leave her London flat without checking the doors were double-locked, and yet this entire castle was open to walk into. Of course, there were probably plenty of people inside who would spot an intruder before they took too much, but it still seemed like an unnecessary risk to take.

'Have you eaten?' the man asked, standing at the open door.

'Um, I had a sandwich a couple of hours ago.'

'Aye or nae? Do you need food?'

Bex cleared her throat. 'Um, no; to be honest, I'm pretty tired, actually. I could do with a bath and bed.'

'All right, well, I'll show you to your room then.'

No *How was your journey?* or *Have you been here before?* He clearly wasn't one for small talk, although to be fair, she wasn't much in the mood for it either. As the old man moved inside, Bex followed, and immediately, she felt all the air escape her lungs.

'This place is huge,' she said.

She'd seen it from the outside, of course, and already knew it was massive, but seeing it like this – the wide-open hall, the vaulted ceilings and the two staircases she could see from where she was standing – was giving her an entirely different perspective. It was colossal.

Bex took a second to look around her, casting her eyes over the heavy tapestries that hung from the walls, dulled with dust. She thought all buildings like this had been turned into hotels or opened to the public as stately homes to visit. But this place had none of the ambience of a hotel or a stately home.

That wasn't to say it wasn't stunning. It was absolutely beautiful, and she could only imagine how it would come to life when it was filled with people, those high-society functions of years gone by. But it felt like it was missing something now.

'Don't dilly-dally. Are you coming or not?'

The man was now over by one of the staircases, all but one of his pack of dogs close on his heels. That last one was that same red Labrador, and it was sticking unusually close to Bex, as if she, and not the man, were its owner.

'Sorry,' she said, picking up her pace to catch up with him. 'How many people live in this house?'

'Well, Horace still comes up twice a week, sometimes more. And young Duncan – well, it seems like he spends more time here than in his bloody lodge. But mostly, it's just me.'

'You?'

'Aye. Me, and the dogs, of course.'

The entire situation was growing more and more confusing. So the groundskeeper lived in the main castle? Where the hell were the owners?

'Sorry,' Bex said, trying her best to sound polite, 'but I didn't even catch your name. Or your role here. Who are you?'

The old man frowned. His already crinkled face crumpled up like a piece of washing that had been forgotten at the bottom of the basket.

'I'm Fergus, Laird of LochDarroch. Who the hell did you think I was?'

Bex swallowed a lump in her throat. There was no way she could answer that question. Telling the laird of this great Scottish castle, who also held all her future career prospects in his hands, that she'd thought he was a homeless person – or, at best, a very scruffy groundskeeper – didn't seem like a great way to make an impression.

'I was just confirming, that's all. It's been a long drive,' she added, smiling broadly, though it did little to alleviate the glower on the old man's face.

'Harrumph,' he grunted before turning around and making his way up the stairs. 'Your room is just up here. And you'll want a good night's sleep. You got a fair heft o' work ahead.'

6

Bex tried to stay on Fergus's heels as he made his way up to the second floor and into the maze of corridors that weaved through the castle, but it was hard not to get distracted. There was just so much to look at.

Massive oil paintings depicting images of the rugged Scottish Highlands were interspersed with ornately gilded mirrors, small portraits and countless vases stacked on intricately carved wooden tables. Fingers crossed he had an inventory of all this stuff for the insurers somewhere that she could use for the accounts, because she had no idea what all this would be worth.

They were a third of the way down the corridor when Fergus stopped by one of the large wooden doors.

'This'll be you,' he said gruffly. 'There's an electric shower in there. Nae point having the water heating on for the whole place when it's just us here. If it gets a bit driech, there's an electric blanket. I know how you southern folk struggle.'

Bex was only half listening and even from the parts she'd heard, she wasn't sure she understood. Driech? Cold, maybe. That would make sense in the context. Still, she didn't ask for clarification. She was too busy staring at the room Fergus had just told her she would be staying in.

It was difficult not to gawp given that it looked like she had just stepped onto the set of *Downton Abbey*. Or maybe *The Tudors*. The space alone was as big as the entire kitchen, dining and living area of her London flat, and the windows had to be at least seven feet tall as they let in the orange-hued evening light. There were heavy red curtains, a marble fireplace and, of course, a massive four-poster bed, complete with sheer drapes around it. This wasn't the type of room you let your accountant sleep in when they were up here on business. This was the type of room royalty stayed in. And given the number of doors they had passed – and the fact that they were on the second floor – it made her think that there were plenty more rooms like this. But Fergus said he lived here alone? That didn't make sense.

'Sorry, did you say you lived here on your own?' Bex asked, sure she must have got the wrong end of the stick.

'Like I said, sometimes I get the laddie from the lodge who comes up here a bit. Uses this room when his water acts up, and I've got a nephew, Kieron. He comes sometimes too. Likes to use the place for his shoot days.'

'Shoot days?' Bex said, vaguely recalling Daisy mentioning something like that when she had been driving.

'Aye. Shoots. Comes up with his friends from London. I hide myself away, but I dinnae suspect you'll be seeing much of him. I've got Nora, too; she comes in an' does the cleaning for me three times a week, so you'll probably see her, but it's best to stay out her way. She's got enough to do without you making even more mess for her.'

'So you and the dogs live here alone?' she said, now certain she had understood that was what he was telling her, just unsure how that was possible. The old man tilted his head to the side.

'That's what I said, isn't it? I 'ope you're better with numbers than with words.' Bex wasn't sure how she was supposed to reply to that, but as it happened, she didn't need to as Fergus carried on speaking. 'I'll 'ave plenty to be gettin' on with in the morning, so I don't expect to see you first thing. But the study is down the stairs. You'll find the paperwork and things in there. Get yourself started.'

With that, he turned around and left, four of his five dogs trotting after him. The one that remained was the same red Labrador as before. Oblivious to Bex until now, said dog had snuck across the room and jumped into the armchair, where she was curled up and feeling most comfortable. Bex was about to tell her that she probably needed to leave, when Fergus reappeared in the room.

'Seems like Ruby's taken a liking to you,' he said before his gaze narrowed on his dog. 'You can stay if you like, but this one's got nae idea where your food is. So, you coming?'

The dog looked between Bex and Fergus as if it was genuinely considering her options, before she leisurely climbed down from the seat and strolled towards her owner. Though rather than going directly towards him, she took a slight detour to nudge her nose into Bex's hand. It was a small moment, but one Bex felt was meant to convey that she would have stayed there with her had it not been for the food issue.

'Daft animal,' Fergus muttered, turning to leave for a second time.

'Go on, Ruby, I'll see you tomorrow,' Bex said, offering the dog a quick rub behind the ears before she finally headed out after Fergus and the rest of the pack. As the animal disappeared

from view, Bex smiled to herself. Even if the old lord was far
from affable, at least she had one friend in the castle.

7

As Bex closed the door, she let out a long sigh before breathing in a lungful of cold, slightly musty air. The entire situation had been completely surreal, and she needed a moment to process it all. One old, bedraggled, and somewhat grumpy man appeared to live in this entire castle by himself. How was that possible? And cleaning three days a week? She had a cleaner once a week for her flat because she despised mopping her floors. Mopping a place like this, especially with five dogs seeming to have free rein, would be a Herculean task. No, she corrected herself. It would be more like that man who had to roll a boulder up a hill every day, wouldn't it?

And speaking of hills.

Now that she had gathered herself, Bex moved away from the door to the other side of the room and not for the first time that day, she felt her breath become stolen by the scenery. The view out of the window was utterly sublime. Even Daisy's home, Wildflower Lock, couldn't compete with this. Rolling hills were covered in constantly changing terrain, from forests to rocky outcrops and lush green fields, and there in the middle of it all was a large, glimmering lake. No, a loch, she corrected herself again. She was definitely looking at a loch.

Birds dipped and dived across the vista as the evening light reflected off the water. She couldn't draw her eyes away from it. Hopefully, the study would have less of an appealing view, she thought. There was no way she'd be able to focus on work if she kept looking outside at something like this. It was only when she yawned so loudly that her jaw clicked that Bex remembered the reason she had asked Fergus to show her straight up here – she was shattered, and that double bed was calling her name.

After shutting the curtains, she crossed the room and let herself flop down. The springs let out a low creak that Bex reciprocated with a satisfied grin of her own. When she'd moved into her flat, she'd bought herself a top-of-the-line, memory foam internal spring support mattress, but it didn't feel anywhere near as soft as this. This was amazing. She wiggled further up so that her whole body was on the bed and stretched her arms out wide, only to find several inches of space between her fingertips and the edges. Work hard, sleep hard. That was going to be her motto for the next two months.

As she lay there staring up at the ceiling, which was an entire piece of artwork on its own, Bex considered having a shower. After all, she'd been stuck in the car all day. And there had been that little incident with walking barefoot through the ford, too. But she knew that a shower would wake her up, and that was the last thing she wanted. So instead, she fired off a quick message to the girls, letting them know she'd made it safely, then stripped off and climbed into bed. She was asleep before her head even hit the monstrously soft pillow.

* * *

Bex was the type of person who needed an alarm. It made no difference that she woke up at the same time every single weekday and had done for the last decade. If she didn't have an alarm, she could almost be guaranteed to sleep in. At least, that was normally the case. It was only when she rolled over in bed, confused by the loud noise that definitely wasn't coming from her phone, that she realised what had happened.

'Seriously,' Bex said, glancing over at the thick curtains, which were absolutely not soundproof. No, she knew that because the entire room was filled with birdsong. Not to mention bird squawks and chirps and any other sound the feathered creatures were capable of making. She thought it was bad at Wildflower Lock, waking up to the dawn chorus, but that felt positively tame compared to the cacophony that was currently drifting through the window.

Bex blinked, stretched out in the bed and rolled over to check the time on her phone. 5.45 a.m.?

'I'm gonna need to get earplugs if you guys are planning on waking me up this early every morning,' she muttered, though there was clearly no chance of the birds either hearing or understanding her.

Groaning as she stretched again, she sat up and swung her legs over the edge of the bed, before staggering over to the window. Maybe she had left it open without knowing. Maybe that was the reason they were so bloody loud. Yet as she pulled the curtains open and stared out of the morning beyond, any thought of shutting off the noise or going back to bed evaporated.

Somehow, the view was even more impressive now, with a delicate morning light stretching across the hills and a soft, gauzy mist hanging low above the loch. Grabbing her phone, she took a quick snap and fired it off to Daisy. Her friend was a painter and would absolutely love this.

With the photo taken and all the curtains open, Bex didn't see any point in climbing back into bed. In hindsight, she was surprised she had fallen asleep so easily. If she would have known that she would be staying in a near-abandoned castle she might have found the idea somewhere between somewhat creepy and mildly terrifying, but she hadn't been the slightest bit nervous going to bed at all. Then again, maybe it was because she had been so tired, or maybe it was just because this room was probably used to visitors like the nephew and... who was the other person? The groundsman, maybe? No, Fergus had said something about a kid, hadn't he? Not that it mattered now. For the next two months, this was going to be her room.

'Right, time to see how hot this electric shower actually is,' she said to herself, grabbing a towel and heading into the bathroom.

Just like the rest of her room, the bathroom was colossal. There was a large, freestanding roll-top bath at one end, a separate shower, a toilet and his-and-hers sinks. An electric towel rail was just beside the door. It was hardly cold, but there was no feeling quite so good as stepping out of the shower and wrapping yourself in a nice warm towel. She hung hers up by the door, crossed the bathroom and stepped into the shower.

Given how elaborate and expensive everything else in the room and bathroom was, Bex was surprised to find a plastic bottle of men's shower gel on the shelf in the shower. It didn't seem like the type of thing Fergus would use, and she couldn't imagine the nephew of the laird going for a cheaper brand either. Still, given that she had left her own washbag in the bedroom, she squirted a blob of gel onto her hand. She was surprised to find it didn't smell that bad at all and a quick look at the label told her it was pine scented. It would definitely do.

Just as Fergus had said, the shower was surprisingly good, and this came from someone who liked their water red hot. As such, it didn't take long before the glass steamed up entirely and for that pine aroma to flood her senses. It was the type of shower she could have stayed in for ages if her stomach wasn't growling loudly. Maybe it hadn't been the best idea to go to bed without a proper meal. She would need to have something now. Both food and a coffee. Then she could get on with her first day at work.

Switching off the water, Bex reached through the cloud of steam to open the glass door, stepped outside, and headed towards her towel.

Why would someone place the towel rail so far away from the shower? she thought as goosebumps rose on her arms. Maybe it was because the room was so big and they didn't want empty spaces, but common sense should have dictated they put it closer than that. With her body dripping and aware of the puddle forming at her feet, she shuffled over towards the towel rail, the heat of the shower long forgotten. When she finally got there, Bex reached out a hand, her fingertips just brushing the soft fabric, when the door swung open.

For a split second, she thought it must have been the wind from the open window, or that maybe it was the dog Ruby who had come up to say good morning, but it took a single blink for her to realise she was very, very wrong.

Standing in the doorway to her bathroom, and unlike her, totally dressed, was a broad man with blue-green eyes and tousled blond hair. And he was staring right at her with his jaw hanging open.

'What the hell are you doing?' Her voice was a shriek as she whipped the towel across herself as quickly as she could, but there was no doubt the man had seen everything. He was standing there, mouth still wide open, cheeks turning redder and redder.

'Oh God, oh God, I'm so sorry, I'm so sorry,' he stammered, raising a hand to shield his eyes, even though Bex was now covered with a towel. 'I didn't think anybody – nobody ever uses – I'm going, I'm going. I was never here. I'm going!'

8

Bex stood there, dumbfounded, as the man backed out of the room, keeping his eyes covered even as he fumbled his way out. A second later, she heard the bedroom door click shut.

What the hell had just happened?

In her shock, she hadn't really taken much in about his appearance, but now, as her heartbeat gradually slowed, an image formed in her mind. He had been good-looking, she realised, and it hadn't just been his green-blue eyes. He'd been tall. Bearded. A quintessential rugged Scot. That was how he'd looked to her, but who the hell was he? The nephew? Her temperature plummeted. Oh God, had Fergus's nephew just seen her in the buff? It certainly seemed like that. Of all the ways to start a job – a job that could control the very outcome of her future career – displaying herself to the boss's nephew did not seem like the best idea.

Bex drew a long breath in then blew it out slowly as she tried to stop herself from going into full panic state. She would just have to pretend it had never happened. Forget she ever saw him. Yes, that would be the easiest thing to do. And he would want to do the same too, wouldn't he? Of course he would. He was the nephew of a lord. That had to be close to royalty or something. There was no chance he'd ever want to admit to walking in on one of his uncle's guests – his accountant no less – naked. Yes, this was just as embarrassing for him, if not more so.

The entire time she was getting dressed, Bex rehearsed through what she was going to say if she saw the nephew again. She would simply act like she hadn't met him before. Never seen him in her life. Then he would do the same, and it would all be as though the incident had never happened. That was what she thought, at least until she stepped out of her bedroom and saw him standing there in the hallway.

Her stomach did something between a flip and a cartwheel, yet before she could even get a word out, like 'let's just pretend that never happened', he was walking straight to her.

'I'm so sorry,' he said, moving from where he'd clearly been leaning against the wall waiting. His cheeks were still a rugged pink, as if the embarrassment had yet to fade, and as he got closer, the colour deepened further, with the blush going all the way up to the top of his ears. Now, without the shock, Bex could take him in a little better and as such, she realised she'd been wrong about her first assumption. He wasn't just good-looking like she'd first thought. He was gorgeous. His eyes were piercing and so unique in colour, while his sandy-blond hair was the same colour as his beard, which was a little longer than anyone's she'd ever dated before. Not that she was thinking of dating him – looking at Fergus's nephew that way was not okay, even if he had seen her naked. She quickly brushed the thought from her mind.

'No one ever normally uses that bathroom,' he said, his thick Scottish accent causing an abnormal fluttering in her belly as it resonated down her spine. 'Fergus lets me use it when the water's gone at the lodge – which is most of the time. I didn't realise you'd be here. He said you were starting work on Tuesday; I just thought... I'm sorry. Very sorry.'

Bex bit down on her bottom lip. In any other situation, she'd have given him an earful about checking before barging into rooms, but this wasn't the right person to do that to. She inhaled deeply in an attempt to steady her pulse, but the effect it had was the exact opposite. Was that pine she could smell? Pine like the shower gel she had just cleaned herself with, only she was certain the aroma was coming from him and not her. God, that smell suited him.

Stop it, Bex, she scolded herself. Pushing her shoulders back, she plastered her most professional smile on her face, then stretched out her hand towards him.

'I'm Rebecca Barker,' she said. 'You must be Kieron.'

The man raised an eyebrow as a slight smirk tugged at his lips. 'Oh no, I am not Kieron. I'm Duncan.'

Duncan? Fergus had mentioned a Duncan, hadn't he? Something about 'the young lad'. In Bex's mind, she'd imagined just that – maybe a thirteen- or fourteen-year-old kid who enjoyed spending time around the castle. This Duncan was definitely not that. Standing at least six foot two, with broad shoulders and a solid stance, he looked 100 per cent man to her. Bex felt heat rise in her cheeks as she tried to quash the thought.

'Sorry, I don't understand. What are you doing here? Where's the lodge?'

'I'm the groundskeeper. I've got a little cottage, the lodge, just round the back of the keep. Look, I really am sorry. Let me make it up to you. Have you had breakfast yet?'

Her stomach growled, answering the question, though Bex hadn't decided if she wanted to go anywhere with him. Sure, he was good-looking, but how did she know he was actually who he said he was? Yesterday when she'd arrived, she'd thought to herself how anyone could just walk into the castle, the way Fergus left it unlocked. Maybe this man pretending to be Duncan had done just that.

'I was just gonna grab a slice of toast and get on with work,' she said.

Duncan's eyebrows rose, and there it was again – that smile, close to a smirk, twisting at the corners of his lips. She wasn't sure she liked it, regardless of how attractive he looked doing it.

'Well, unless you brought some bread with you, you're going to be out of luck. Fergus keeps nothing in the house.'

Bex scoffed. 'I'm sure he's got bread.'

'He doesn't,' Duncan said, without batting an eyelid. 'The only thing he has a decent supply of is whisky. Occasionally, he'll buy a nice bottle of red wine to have at home too, but for his meal, he prefers to support the village. And it's a habit I've kinda fallen into now too. I have breakfast at Maggie's, lunch at the Thistle. Normally. I like to mix it up now and then.'

As Bex mulled his comment over, she studied his face. She'd had plenty of men give her incredibly lame reasons to try to get her on dates before. There was that time a colleague insisted there was a Tube strike and that she'd be quicker going with him in his car; then he'd suggested they stop for dinner and make a night of it. That was when she realised the Tube was running perfectly well after all. She'd even had men she didn't know approach her on girls' nights out, insisting they could show her a 'better time' and trying to buy her a drink.

Clearly, this Duncan thought he was smooth and that she'd fall for his plan of trying to take her out for breakfast, but that wasn't going to happen.

'Well, thank you for the offer, but I'm fine,' she said.

He frowned. 'Really, I'm not playing any games with you. If

you need something to eat and you don't want dog food – which is the only other thing Fergus has plenty of – then it's a mile and a half into the village. Or you could grab a lift with me now.' He sounded sincere. There was no doubt about that, but Bex still wasn't falling for it.

'Well, have a nice drive to the village, Duncan,' Bex said, plastering on her best no-bull smile. 'If you are the groundskeeper, like you say, then I'm sure I'll see you around. Ideally, not in my bathroom next time.'

9

How the hell was there no food in a home this size? For the last forty minutes, that was the only question Bex had been asking herself. How was there not just a box of cornflakes or Weetabix somewhere? There was a kitchen bigger than most restaurants, not one, but two walk-in pantries, and enough shelves and cupboards to store her lifetime's belongings three times over. Yet so far, all Bex had found was dog food. Sacks of dried biscuits filled the pantry floor, along with tinned food on the shelves, and then, in the freezer, where she'd hoped to come across a loaf of frozen bread, there was only raw meat, of which several packets more were defrosting in the fridge. There was also half a pack of butter, an open jar of cranberry sauce and a bottle of vinegar. None of which could be made into any kind of meal.

As she stood there in the large kitchen, Bex contemplated whether she could just push through until lunchtime. But she knew how hangry she got, and the last thing she wanted was to face the study and get her first glance of the task ahead on an empty stomach. No, that wouldn't work at all. As her jaw ground together, she didn't know what she was more annoyed about. The fact that her day was already derailed before it had even started, or that the irritatingly attractive Duncan had been right. Yes, that definitely made matters even more frustrating.

Trying to shake off the cloud that had well and truly settled on her shoulders, Bex went back upstairs and grabbed her boots. She needed to head into the village and driving there would be the quickest option, but she suspected that once she had actually got started on the job, she was unlikely to get much free time, which was a shame considering how beautiful the scenery was. Walking while she had the time to do so seemed like the most sensible option. Besides, it gave her a chance to fill the girls in on her latest development.

'Oh my God! This is fate!' Claire exclaimed from one corner of the screen. 'It's just like Daisy and Theo, walking in on him in the shower. It's meant to be.'

'No, it's absolutely not,' Bex replied. 'And he walked in on me. Let's remember that. Surely he should have seen the bag on the floor in the bedroom – that should have been a sign that the bathroom was occupied.'

'So other than the ruggedly handsome groundsman, have you met anyone else?' Daisy asked.

'I didn't say he was ruggedly handsome,' Bex protested.

'No, but he is, right? The way you keep talking about him makes it sound like he's ruggedly handsome.'

'I keep talking about him because he walked in on me in the shower. And no, I haven't met anyone else yet, apart from Fergus, the Laird, and his dogs. The dogs are nice.'

Before Bex could continue, she heard a voice calling for coffee on Daisy's end. Daisy crinkled her nose. 'Sorry, I've got to go.'

'Yeah, me too,' Claire said. 'I need to get Amelia to school.

But fill us in on the rest of the day soon, okay? Especially any more chance encounters with attractive Scottish men.'

Bex rolled her eyes. 'Love you both,' she said, before hanging up and slipping her phone back into her pocket.

She was grateful she'd packed her boots, that was for sure, as the dew from the grass seeped into the hem of her jeans. Had she been wearing her trainers, her feet would have likely been soaked through. Either that or she would have been forced to stick to the path, and there was no chance she wanted to do that.

There was just too much to see. Too much to take photos of. Every direction offered something different, from the way the light dappled through the branches to the manner in which the sun reflected off the grass. And then there were the birds. Sure, she had hated them for waking her up so damn early, but she could hardly blame them. It was a million miles from even the greenest of London's parks. Of course they wanted to sing every morning if this was what they woke up to. It was something special. A place that seemed untouched from the modern world, and she suspected she'd appreciate it even more if she weren't so hungry.

By the time the village came into view, her stomach was growling angrily, but once again, Bex was slowed by the sight that met her. Last night, when she'd driven in, exhausted and fed up after a series of delays, she hadn't appreciated just how lovely the place was. If her room at the castle belonged in a period drama, then this village looked like it could be the setting for some cosy romance film. The type where the female main character packed up her big city life to take on some new challenge in the middle of nowhere only to fall in love with the most eligible bachelor in the village. She laughed at the thought. Those women obviously didn't have a massive promotion waiting for them when they got back to their real life.

Maintaining a steady amble, Bex took in as much as she could. The main street was easily identifiable, with cobblestones stretching up the hill and buildings of all different heights and styles giving it a charmingly haphazard feel. She already knew from what Duncan had said that there were places to get food at this time of day, and her plan was to go to whichever one she found first, but as she approached what appeared to be a café, the door swung open and out stepped a now familiar figure.

'No luck finding any food in the house?' Duncan asked, the slightest hint of a smirk tugging at the corner of his mouth.

Bex didn't bother responding; instead, she glowered at him. Annoyingly, Daisy had been spot on – he was ruggedly handsome, and he looked even more so here. It was like his hair and skin glowed in the sunlight.

'Well, I thought that might be the case, so I bought you a few bits and pieces,' he said, lifting a bag in his hand. 'Nothing too exciting. Croissants. Bread. A couple of pieces of fruit. You can take them now, if you want, or I can put them in the kitchen for when you get back?'

Bex's eyes narrowed. He was winding her up, wasn't he? He hadn't really bought her breakfast. Not after she had insisted on ignoring the advice he had given her.

'I guess this is your way of apologising for walking in on me?' she said, placing her hands on her hips. His smirk widened.

'No, the apology I gave you outside your room was my way of apologising for that,' he replied smoothly. 'This is breakfast. Food. I do believe you still have that "south of the border", don't you?'

He clearly thought he was amusing, but he didn't seem to understand the concept of hangry. That cute little smirk might work on other women, but she had dated hundreds of men just like him. And that wasn't an exaggeration. One night she had done a two-hundred-person speed dating event, with a hundred men and a hundred women, and she had left with one firm conclusion: the ones who believed they were attractive were the ones you needed to be most wary of. And there was no way Duncan didn't know how attractive he was, with those massive eyes of his that she inadvertently found herself looking in to.

With a slight shift, she cleared her throat. 'Well, whatever the reason, I'm perfectly capable of getting my own food, and if you don't mind, that's what I'm going to do.'

She had hoped that her words, matched with her tone, would have been enough to make Duncan move out of the way so she could get into the café, but he continued to stand there, looking at her. Although rather than smirking, a single frown line had formed between his brows.

'Look, I'm sorry for the rough introduction,' he said. 'We clearly got off on the wrong foot. Maybe we can start over? I'm Duncan. I hear you're working up at the castle.'

He stretched out his hand and raised an eyebrow, signifying the ball was now in her court. Bex felt the muscles in her jaw twitch. There was no way she couldn't take it. Not without looking like she was being petulant. And that wasn't who she was at all. With a slight sigh, she lifted her arm, ready to shake his hand, yet as his fingertips brushed against her palm, a static jolt shot through her skin, strong enough to make her heart stutter. Her eyes snapped up and met his gaze, and from the way his pupils had grown, she was certain he had felt it too.

'I... I...' She wanted to say something, wanted to step back, but her mouth had grown uncharacteristically dry, and her feet refused to respond. As for her hand, rather than moving away, it had remained there and was now enclosed in his grip. Was all his skin this warm? she wondered. What would it feel like if he moved his hand to the back of her neck, or...

'Right!' Bex jumped back, pulling her hand from his grip and putting as much distance between them as she could in one leap. 'I... Food. Need food,' she stammered, pointing at the café door, wishing words would leave her mouth in more than single syllables. She half expected Duncan to respond with some quip, or at least that smirk he had shown her before, but he remained standing there, his hand frozen mid-air, as if he hadn't been able to move either.

'Right. Sure... food,' he said, his eyes still locked on hers. Somehow, it was even more unnerving than when he'd seen her naked, and she wouldn't have thought that was possible.

Unable to take it any longer, she pushed open the café door, not even checking if anyone was behind it, and rushed inside. All she needed was to get away from Duncan, his electric hand-shake and that penetrating gaze.

As she heard the door click shut behind her, a gasp of relief escaped her lungs. What the heck was that? Lightning in a bottle? A spark? All those things romance novels tried to make you believe were real, just to sell more copies. That was all she'd ever thought it was. And yet, for the first time in her life, she had felt it.

No, she told herself. She hadn't. It was just tiredness and stress. Either that or it was static, caused by the weather. That happened, didn't it? Of course it did. Lightning happened because of the atmosphere, and they were up in the Highlands. Yes, it was just a weather effect.

Slowly taking in her surroundings of white tables and the aroma of freshly baked goods, Bex took a deep breath. She was fine. Whatever had happened, she was completely fine. She was here to do a job, and Duncan would not interfere with that. Actually, if she had it her way, she wouldn't see him again at all.

Feeling like she'd once again gathered some composure, she headed over to the counter.

There were two women behind it. One was an elderly lady who looked frail enough to be knocked over by a strong gust of wind yet somehow was managing to carry several trays of baked goods, and the other, who was around Bex's age, had auburn hair and perfectly winged eyeliner.

'Hi,' Bex said, her voice coming out more breathily than she'd expected. 'Can I have a large cappuccino, please? Double shot. And a food menu.'

The younger woman tilted her head to the side, her gaze fixed on Bex. 'Sure you can,' she said. 'But first you're going to have to tell me what's going on between you and my step-brother.'

10

Bex wanted to think she had misheard the woman. After all, she had barely recovered from the static shock spark thing, but she knew she hadn't, just like she knew there was only one person the woman could have been talking about. Once again, her throat felt strangely tight, and she struggled to get out any sound.

'Duncan?' she managed finally. 'Duncan's your brother?'

The woman's smile was wide and mischievous. 'Stepbrother. Which I believe gives me extra right to stick my nose in, even when he definitely doesn't want me to.'

'Oh, well, he and I only just met this morning. Not that there's anything going on with us. At all. Like I said, we just met. Well, not just then, but sort of just then. I mean, we obviously just saw each other then.' Bex wanted to scream at herself. Why the hell had she lost all ability to speak? She was the person the bosses brought out when they needed someone to nail a presentation. Someone who could talk with absolute clarity and conviction regardless of the situation. Maybe the air was just thinner up here. Maybe that was why her thoughts were so confused.

'Okay...' The woman spoke slowly, as if she was needing time to process what Bex had just said. Not that Bex could even make any sense of it herself. 'Right, well, regardless of when you met, I'm gonna need to lay some ground rules. I know he might come across as all charming and like he's up for a good time, but that's not the type of guy he is. He's dealing with a serious broken heart.'

'Oh,' Bex said. She wasn't sure what else she was meant to say, although the woman didn't seem too bothered by her minimal answers. Instead, she picked up a jug of milk and went over to the coffee machine, where she carried on talking.

'Yup. Bad broken heart. And I'm guessing from the accent that you're not from around here.'

'No, I'm from London.'

The girl gave a little laugh. 'Of course you are. Trust me, there is no way Duncan can deal with some rebound fling with a high-flying businesswoman who's here for a holiday. So can you do me a favour and just steer clear of him? Please?'

As she placed the cup of coffee down in front of Bex, the woman's eyes, filled with pain and worry for her stepbrother, met hers. Bex felt a sudden warmth towards the young woman. She got what it was like to be protective of the people you loved, and this woman clearly thought the world of her stepbrother. It took guts to stand up for people like that – even though Bex suspected Duncan would hate to know she was doing it. Still, there was one thing that Bex needed to correct her on.

'I'm actually here for work, rather than a holiday,' she said. 'But don't worry, I have no intention of getting involved with anyone while I'm here.'

'Work?' The woman sprinkled chocolate onto the top of

Bex's drink. 'That sounds interesting. We don't get many people from London working here. What is it you're doing?'

Bex wasn't sure how much she was meant to share about her role up at the castle, but in a small village like this, she suspected that news travelled fast enough.

'I'm working at the castle,' she said.

The woman's eyes widened. 'With Fergus?'

'Yes.'

With the jug still in her hand, the young woman pressed her lips together as if she was suppressing a grin. 'Well, that must be an experience. And speaking of the devil...'

Bex turned her head towards the door, which had just opened. Fergus stalked in, surrounded by his five dogs, one of which made a beeline straight for Bex.

It was no wonder that she'd mistaken him for a homeless man, she thought. It was early morning, but he looked no better now than he had last night. His shirt was a different colour, but it was completely creased, while his pockets bulged with dog treats that peeked out of the top. For a split second, he looked as though he was about to smile when his eyes landed on Bex. His mouth dropped, and a deep scowl creased his forehead.

'What are you doing here?' he said. 'I thought you'd be at work already. I'm not paying you to sit around and drink coffee all day.'

11

Bex didn't get yelled at by bosses. She was the person who bosses held up as an exemplary example on how to do everything. Either that or she was the one who did the yelling at the less senior members of staff. And yet there was Fergus, glowering at her. The feeling was not one she liked.

She opened her mouth, ready to apologise and explain the situation, when the woman cut in.

'Oh, stop being ridiculous, Fergus. It's eight thirty in the morning. Sit down, I'll bring you your usual to go.' As she passed Bex, the woman flashed a smile. 'I'm Lorna, by the way,' she said. 'You take a seat. I'll just grab you that menu.'

Bex wasn't exactly sure she wanted to stay and eat in the same place as her employer, especially when he seemed so grumpy and miserable. But she was sure that Lorna had just said he was getting his order to go, and she didn't want to be stuck with him on the long walk back over to the castle. Though, as she took a seat, she had a now-familiar shadow.

'Ruby, isn't it?' she said, leaning down and stroking the dog before hushing her voice. 'You're going to get me in trouble if you keep following me like this. I need to make a good impression with Fergus. Go on. Go back to him. I'll see you when I'm back at the castle.' The dog tilted her head to the side, placed a paw momentarily on Bex's knee, then turned around and headed back to Fergus. She knew a couple of cafés back home that allowed you to bring your dog in, provided they were well behaved, but she couldn't imagine anywhere this small letting someone come in with five such large animals and not a lead in sight. But then, maybe if you were the Laird you got to make up your own rules.

'He really is a case of "his bark is worse than his bite",' Lorna said after Fergus had left. She had brought Bex a menu, just as she'd said, but rather than leaving it on the table so that Bex could choose what she wanted to order, she had taken a seat with her. 'He's just not very good at the initial getting-to-know-you part, that's all. Trust me, Fergus is an absolute softy. I bet within a week you'll have him eating out of your hand.'

Bex wasn't sure that was true, and she wasn't entirely sure she wanted Fergus eating out of her hand either. That didn't seem like the best approach for a professional relationship. But she smiled politely all the same.

'I'm just here to get work done,' she said.

'Right. Of course.' Lorna looked as if she was about to move, only to hesitate and change her mind. 'Look, I'm guessing if they've brought you up from London to work at the castle, you've probably got a lot on and not much free time. But I'm meeting a couple of friends tonight for a drink if you'd like to join us. I mean, I don't know how long you're staying, but if it's just a few days—'

'Two months,' Bex interrupted. 'That's how long my boss assumed the project is going to take.'

'Two months?' Lorna's eyebrows rose. 'Well, if that's the case, you are definitely going to need people to go for a drink with. If you fancy it at all.'

Bex was here to work, not to make friends, and the sooner she got the job done, the sooner she would be back in London. She knew that. As such, she was about to give Lorna a more polite version of her initial reaction to the offer, but before she did, she stopped herself. Yes, Bex was hardworking, but she was also a people person, and she was so used to having Daisy and Claire there on call whenever she needed them. Not to mention people at the office she could grab a drink with after a hard day at work. The thought of spending the entire two months in the castle with only Fergus and Duncan – who she wasn't even sure she wanted to be near at all – for company was enough to make her rethink her reply.

'That would be really nice,' she said. 'Thank you. Drinks sounds great.'

Lorna beamed. She clearly hadn't expected Bex to say yes. 'All right, why don't I take your number and I'll message you? We'll probably meet at the White Hart later, but it depends on Eilidh and Niall.'

'Thank you,' Bex said, suddenly feeling immensely grateful for the invitation. She had always suspected that small villages like this could be a bit insular and unwelcoming to strangers, but Lorna didn't seem that way at all. 'Oh, and if you don't want to trek up here for breakfast or deal with the pre-packaged stuff at the supermarket, I've got some frozen croissants and things you can take back with you. They go beautifully in the Aga. If you don't believe me, you can always ask Duncan – he's constantly stealing things from the freezer here. Actually, if you see him, you can tell him I know he's constantly stealing things from the freezer.'

Bex let out a light chuckle while trying to stop her cheeks

from colouring at Duncan's name. 'Thank you,' she said, at which point Lorna pushed back her chair and stood up from the table.

'Well, that's enough chatting for now, I better get on with work.' She moved to go, only to look back. 'Sorry, I didn't even get your name.'

'Rebecca,' Bex said, only to correct herself. 'Bex. Bex Barker.'

'Well, Bex Barker, in case no one has said it yet, welcome to LochDarroch. I think you're going to have a great time here.'

12

Forty minutes later, Bex was leaving the café with Lorna's phone number and a large bag of fresh and frozen pastries – definitely enough for breakfast for the next few days. Lorna had also lent her a large tote bag to carry everything in and made her a second large cappuccino to take away, just in case Fergus was out of coffee at the castle. If that was the case, Bex knew she would need to do some serious shopping, but her arms were already laden down and she was aware that it was now almost nine thirty and at some point she really had to start work. Yet as she stepped from the café onto the pavement, she stopped.

'Really?' she said, looking at the figure sitting just a few feet away from her, tongue lolling from her mouth as the tempo of her tail wagging increased. There was no denying which dog Bex was looking at. As such, she scanned around her, searching for signs of Fergus or the other dogs, but while she saw a couple of people in wax jackets, none of them were the Laird and all the dogs she saw were on leashes. She wasn't even sure Fergus's dogs knew what a leash was.

As she stood there, staring at the pair of big amber eyes, Bex contemplated what she was meant to do. Should she just leave her? That didn't seem safe. It wasn't a particularly busy road, but it was a road, nonetheless.

Keeping a careful hold of her very full takeaway coffee, Bex turned back around and opened the door to the café.

'Hey, everything all right?' Lorna asked.

'I'm not sure,' Bex replied. 'Fergus's dog – Ruby, I think it is – is just sitting outside. But I can't see any sign of Fergus or the other dogs.'

'Huh,' Lorna said, offering a quick shrug before she crossed the café, then poked her head out of the door to the dog sitting out there.

'Is that normal?' Bex asked, having been able to gauge very little from Lorna's response.

Again, her new friend replied with a slight shrug. 'He gives them a pretty free rein, but I've never seen one just sitting here.'

'Well, should we ring someone? Ring Fergus?'

Lorna crinkled her nose. 'You're walking back, aren't you? See if she'll go with you. If she won't, you can tell Fergus when you get back. Or call me, and I'll drop her home.'

It seemed like a sensible suggestion, but Bex still wasn't sure. She was used to walking dogs. Daisy had adopted a stray called Johnny, and she would often look after him while they went away, but Johnny knew her. She had only met this dog yesterday.

'Ruby?' she said tentatively, tapping her thigh lightly as she tried not to dislodge the bag on her shoulder. Immediately, the dog was on her feet and standing to heel by Bex.

Lorna let out an impressed low whistle. 'Well, I think you've got this,' she said. 'But just text me if she doesn't get home.'

'Right,' Bex said. Frozen pastries, a drink date for tonight and a dog. This definitely wasn't the first trip into the village she'd imagined.

As she headed back to the castle, Ruby remained just three feet from her side. Her stride was perfectly in time with Bex and the few times Bex stopped to readjust her bag, Ruby did the same, halting immediately and waiting before Bex started walking again. It was as if the dog wanted to remain close to her, but was also giving her a little bit of space, in case Bex didn't want the same.

As they approached the woodland outside the castle, Bex considered calling Daisy again. She wanted to tell her friend about the new introductions she had made – both Lorna and Ruby – and the fact that she had plans for the evening. But she hesitated. The last thing she wanted was to be ringing Daisy every thirty minutes with updates on her life. Daisy had a business to run, after all. Besides, by tonight, she'd probably have a lot more to share. At least she'd know what the job entailed.

She turned the door handle, unsurprised it was left unlocked, but despite having Ruby at her side, the place felt empty. There was something about the way the air whipped through the hallway that made her think no one was inside. Still, she called out just in case. 'Duncan? Fergus?'

Silence echoed around the hallway, confirming her suspicion, though as she glanced at the large grandfather clock in the hallway, her stomach dropped. How was it already ten thirty? She could never have imagined starting work at this time of day, but between Lorna and Ruby, not to mention the unexpected morning walk, she had lost time of everything. Still, she could always work through lunch. Or skip it altogether to make up the hours.

She headed first to the kitchen, to place the frozen items in the freezer, before returning to the main hall, where Ruby had remained waiting for her.

'Which room did he say it was?' she said, looking down at

the dog. Labradors were supposed to be intelligent, and from the way Ruby had responded to her commands on the walk, she could tell that was true. Unfortunately, that intelligence didn't seem to stretch far enough to tell Bex where she was meant to go. 'I guess I should just start looking for the study then, shouldn't I?' she said.

Ruby was on her feet and wagging her tail. Apparently, Bex was going to have company for this, too.

The first room she came across was clearly a dining room, with a massive table down the centre that must've seated at least twenty people. The next was filled with armchairs, sofas and a large fireplace. Bex hovered in the doorway. There was something about this room that felt lived in. The way the armchair was tilted towards the fire, and the blanket strewn over the back of it. Not to mention the half-full bottle of whisky placed on a side table. If she had to place a bet, then this was where Fergus liked to spend most of his time.

Closing the door behind her, she carried on her search.

'This place has its own library?' she murmured as she opened another door. 'How the hell...'

She shook her head. She could easily lose the entire morning just wandering through the house, looking at the different rooms. But that wasn't what she was here to do.

Finally, she found the door to the left of the staircase. Having checked almost every other space downstairs, she was almost certain this was the study.

'Well, let's see how bad this is,' she said, pushing the heavy door open.

The moment she stepped inside, her stomach plummeted.

13

She had never seen anything like it. Well, maybe in her nightmares, but not in real life. It was the study – she could just about tell that much from the large desk beneath the window, though almost all of it was buried under a sea of paper. Notebooks, paper pads, loose sheets. There was a computer in the corner, or at least she thought there was an entire computer, as she could only make out the top of the monitor; everything below had been swallowed up by yet more notebooks.

Three filing cabinets stood beside one of the bookshelves. They were the nicest filing cabinets Bex had ever seen, gunmetal with dark leather trim along the front and sides, but any charm was overshadowed by their chaotic state. The drawers were halfway open, with papers spilling out at all angles.

'They can't be serious,' Bex muttered, moving cautiously towards the desk.

She picked up a piece of paper – a printed receipt for £350 – but it was faded, and where it was from was anyone's guess as the logo at the top was covered in what appeared to be a coffee stain. She shuffled a few steps to the left, picked up another faded receipt, this one handwritten, and then a large black note-book. It was the kind of accountant's ledger used decades ago, with neat columns for numbers to track everything in. But the printed neat lines were where the order ended. Traditionally, black ink meant money coming in, and red meant money going out. But here, there were black, red, blue, green – even purple – scribbles along the margins.

'What the hell is purple supposed to mean?' She could feel a tightness constricting her throat.

Nigel hadn't been joking about this being a big job. But two months? She'd need two months just to impose some order on the place, let alone start on the actual accounts. What this office needed was a goddamn house clearance, not an accountant.

'Who the hell writes in purple?' she said again, loudly this time, angrily slamming the ledger closed.

'My late wife Winny was a fan of different colours,' came a voice behind her.

Bex spun around. There, standing in the doorway, was Fergus. His scowl was still in place, although softened by a look of sadness in his eyes, which he swallowed down before he nodded his head towards Ruby. 'Looks like this one has taken a liking to you.'

'I'm sorry, I'm so sorry,' Bex stammered. 'I didn't mean to offend you.'

He huffed. 'No, no offence taken. No point lying about it – I know what bad shape it's in.'

'Yeah, it's not great,' Bex said, not sure how else to word it herself.

'So, do you think you can get it sorted for me?' he asked, before shuffling inwards. 'There's a computer in here some-where – not sure if you've seen it. My nephew Kieron insisted I have one. He thinks it works. I'll be honest, he's the one who set it up, and I haven't touched it since, but... he's good with these things.'

There was an optimism to Fergus's voice. A hope. Almost like Bex would sweep in and be able to fix it all with a wave of her magic accounting wand.

Bex nodded. 'I've got a laptop I can use for most of it,' she said, like the old computer was the biggest of their problems.

She was half-tempted to suggest hiring a house clearance team, but that wouldn't help anyone right now. She needed to get through this herself. Nigel's words echoed in her head. It wouldn't be easy, but it would be worth it. Well, he hadn't been joking about the first bit. Whether it would be worth it or not was irrelevant to her. She just had to get through it.

'Well, I was going to take the dogs for a walk,' Fergus said. 'Head down to the loch and give my sister a ring. Unless, of course, you want my help in here?'

Bex shook her head. From her experience, working with people's accounts was a little like helping them move out of their houses. They didn't just see the numbers, they saw the stories behind those numbers, and as such, a simple question like 'do you remember what you spent this on?' could end up in a twenty-minute monologue about the time they went on holiday and saw a python, or some other such unnecessary tale. For now, she needed to get to grips with what was there herself.

'Maybe later, if that's okay,' she replied.

Fergus nodded, then moved to the doorway. 'You coming with me?' he said to Ruby. The dog slumped down onto her belly, at which he let out a sad chuckle. 'Well, I think she's yours now.'

Bex tried to reciprocate the smile, but there was something so sad about the situation. Not just the amount of work she had to do, but this whole place. This empty castle. Fergus here alone. At least he had his sister and nephew. That was something.

Fergus turned to leave, but before he left, he paused, looking back at her.

'It wasn't always this bad,' he said softly. 'It's just... when you get old, you start putting off the things you don't care about so much. And I'm very old now, and paperwork, as you can see, is something I don't care about too much.'

Bex felt another pang of sympathy for the old man. A place this size probably had an endless list of things that needed doing. It made sense that he'd neglect the paperwork. But that didn't change the fact that she was the one who had to deal with it now. Meaning, the sooner she got started, the better.

14

The chime of the grandfather clock in the hallway sounded again. It felt like every ten minutes it needed to announce how quickly time was passing – and how little Bex was managing to get done.

She'd decided to start with the desk. It seemed to have more space, and a fair amount of rubbish, too. Flyers, notes, bank statements, statements from old insurance companies dating back ten years – things she could file away and not worry too much about. She hoped that, once she'd cleared some space on the desk, she'd be able to think a little more clearly. But it felt never-ending, like every time she moved one piece of paper, two more multiplied in its place. She counted the clock chimes, unsure whether it had been four or five strikes, and was contemplating finding her phone to check what the time was when there was a knock on the door.

She had been half expecting Fergus to pop in, possibly around lunchtime, to see how she was doing, but there had been no sign of him. And she was grateful. Any conversation meant time away from the task, and she didn't have any time to spare.

Even if it had just been ten minutes. Rather than taking any form of lunch break, and having no luck locating any coffee in the castle, she'd polished off her stone-cold cappuccino and shoved her second croissant of the day into her mouth, the end of which she had given to Ruby, who'd managed to find a clear spot over by the window and had spent the entire day basking in the sun there. Now, though, as the knock resounded through the air, the dog lifted her head.

'Yes, come in,' called Bex. It felt silly saying come in to Fergus. After all, it was his home and his office, but when the door opened, standing there – unexpectedly – was Duncan. Memories of that static shock that had sparked through her fingers flashed in her mind, and she tried to quash them as quickly as possible.

'Duncan,' she said, keeping her voice as neutral as possible. 'Is everything okay? If you're looking for Fergus, I'm not sure where he is. He said he was taking the dogs for a walk, but that was about six hours ago.'

'Sounds about right,' Duncan said, chuckling. 'Walking the dogs is basically Fergus's reason for doing nothing.' At the mention of the dogs, he looked at Ruby. 'You got yourself a buddy?'

'Apparently so.'

He let out a small laugh, with such a deep resonance, Bex could feel her entire stomach turning to butterflies at the sound. What the hell was wrong with her? Was it the thought of not going on any dates for the next two months that was causing her to find Duncan so blooming attractive? That had to be it. It couldn't be because he was actually attractive, could it? And it definitely wasn't because of that deep pine aroma that was emanating from him even now.

With a slight yelp, she bit the inside of her cheeks. This was

not what she did. Whatever was going on with her, she needed
to get a grip. But it was really damn hard. There was just something about his smile that made it impossible to think about
anything else.

'Are you okay?' Duncan asked. Concern flashed on his face
as he stepped further into the study.

'Yes, fine,' Bex replied, internally cursing herself yet again in
his presence. 'Just my legs have gone a little numb. You know,
from sitting so long.'

'Right,' Duncan said. His eyes lingered on her, like he was
expecting her to say more, but her throat was growing inexplicably dry.

'Like I said, Fergus isn't here,' she repeated, hoping that he
would take the hint and leave.

'That's okay. I came to see you. I brought you a little present.'

A present? Bex's heart hitched.

'Nothing too exciting,' he said, stretching out his hand, palm
open. In the centre was a brass key. 'It's to lock your bedroom
door,' he said. 'To avoid any other... embarrassing incidents.'

Bex stood up and walked over to him.

'Right,' she said before tentatively taking the key from his
hand, careful not to let her fingers brush his, in case it had the
same effect as last time. 'Thank you, I appreciate it. Though
what are you going to do for hot water now if the lodge still isn't
working?'

He shrugged, then grinned. 'It's fine. I'm sure I can scrounge
a shower here or there.'

Was he talking about other women? Probably. Yes, he probably had half the women in the village on speed dial, all
desperate to offer him the use of his shower. Her mind was
wandering, envisioning the queue of eager young ladies lining
up with towels to hold out to him, when he spoke again.

'Actually, there was something else I wanted to ask you too.'

She looked up to find the blue-green eyes staring straight into her.

'Yes?' Bex's pulse ticked faster and faster. What was it about those damn eyes? Not to mention his thick Scottish accent? She wouldn't go as far as to say it made her knees weak, but it was certainly doing something. Unless there was an altitude issue in the castle, too. She hadn't felt it before, but then she had been sitting down for most of the day. Maybe it was standing up that was causing her to have this light-headedness. Tonight, she was going to google it, she decided, although for now, she was sidetracked by the slight shift in Duncan's posture. Almost like he was nervous. He cleared his throat before finally carrying on.

'I was just wondering if you'd like to go for a drink later. You know, as another apology. I feel like I owe you it. And it would give you a chance to see a wee more of the village. And maybe a better side of me, too?'

Nope, she was wrong. Her knees really had gone weak. How the hell did he make the word 'wee' sound gruff? Bex took a deep breath in, but tried to appear casual about it. Did she want to go for a drink with the excessively attractive Scotsman? Absolutely. But was she going to? No.

Dozens of reasons as to why that would be an absolutely terrible idea flashed through her mind. First, he had said it was a drink to see a 'better side' of him. Whether it had been intentional or not, she had read that comment as laden with innuendo and, given that they both worked at the castle, a terrible idea. It literally went against her only rule of dating, which was not to get involved with someone at work. At least half a dozen colleagues had asked her out during her decade at the firm and she had turned them all down. Even the ones she'd actually liked, because she was a woman who didn't let a man interfere with her career, and it didn't matter how professional you were, workplace dating affected how you did your job. And while she wasn't working with Duncan in the same way as her colleagues in London, it was still too close to be comfortable. Then there was the fact that Duncan was going through a massive heart-break. Rebound guys were always a disaster. And then, to add to that, his stepsister, who Bex already liked even after one short meeting, had warned her quite firmly against dating him. The last thing she wanted to do was ostracise the only person she had made a connection with in the village. No, attractiveness aside, she would not be going for a drink with Duncan.

'Actually,' she said, grateful to have an excuse that wasn't just a direct refusal, 'I've already made plans tonight. I'm having drinks with your stepsister.'

'Lorna?' His eyebrows rose, and a small smile lifted his lips. Clearly, from his reaction to her name, he was as fond of his sister as she was of him. 'Well, I'm sure you'll have a lot of fun. Just do me a favour, will you?' he said, that damn accent causing yet more butterflies to swarm inside her.

'What's that?' Bex asked.

'Don't believe anything she says about me.' With that, he flashed her one perfect grin and disappeared out of the study.

Bex let out a long sigh. Why did she get the feeling that working here was going to be a whole lot harder than she'd anticipated? And it had nothing to do with the state of the study.

15

Bex continued working for several hours after Duncan left, and it was only when her phone buzzed, showing a message from Lorna saying they were all at the White Hart, that she realised how late it was. Hurriedly, she went upstairs, had a quick shower and changed her clothes.

She reached the bottom of the staircase, ready to head out the door, when a voice boomed out from the room Bex had spotted the whisky and angled armchair in earlier that day.

'You sound in a right rush, thundering down those stairs,' Fergus called. 'Where you off to? Or do I nae wanna know?'

Bex poked her head around the door and found him sitting in the armchair, all five dogs at his feet, although Ruby immediately started wagging her tail.

'Sorry,' Bex said. 'I'm just late in meeting Lorna for a drink.'

'Lorna, aye, she's a good lass.'

Bex wondered if this might be the first compliment she had heard Fergus give someone, and she waited, half expecting him to continue. But there was nothing. Just silence. Almost like he wasn't sure how you were supposed to keep conversation going.

Bex shifted her feet a little. She didn't want to be rude, but she was well aware that she was already late and this somewhat awkward conversation was only making her later.

'I should—'

'Sorry again—'

The pair spoke directly over one another, and a flash of embarrassment rolled through Bex.

'You want to get off,' Fergus said, waving his hand. 'Dinnae let me keep you.'

'It's fine,' Bex said, feeling an unexpected surge of guilt at leaving the old man in this massive castle on his own, even though she suspected he'd been living that way for years on end.

'Aye, well. I also... I also wanted to say sorry again about the mess of things,' Fergus said.

Sorry again. Bex almost felt her jaw drop. She wasn't sure she had heard him say sorry once yet. He had warned her it was a state, but that wasn't exactly the same thing, was it?

She let out a slight chuckle. 'I'll just make sure I bill you for every minute worked. And that includes binning old Mars bar wrappers. Seems you rather like those.'

She had meant the comment as a joke and had assumed he would take it as one, but instead, his face hardened.

'Well, I dinnae wanna keep you any longer.'

'Right,' Bex said, feeling unusually guilty. 'I guess I'll see you in the morning.'

'Aye, and early this time please,' he called.

As she walked out the room, she found herself shaking her head. It was safe to say, no part of her first day working in Scotland had been anything like what she'd expected. And the day wasn't even over yet.

16

Bex knew that driving was the sensible option. It meant she wouldn't be able to get too drunk and make a bad impression, and it also meant that she wouldn't stay too late, because as much as she wanted to have fun, she still had a lot of work to do. Her third reason for driving was less optimistic, but if she had been wrong about Lorna, and she wasn't as nice as first impressions had seemed, or perhaps her friends were not the type of people she could feel comfortable around, then she would be able to get out of there quick-sharp. Fingers crossed that wasn't something she had to worry about.

Still, as she parked up the car and walked towards the pub, an unexpected wave of nerves hit her. It had been a long time since she'd made new friends. Her closest friends were the ones she'd grown up with, and she had several at the office as well. She only ever really met new people when someone joined her firm, and when that happened, they were normally the nervous one, hoping they would fit in. This was entirely different; she was the odd one out, joining an established group. Yet the moment she pushed the door open and Lorna saw her, Duncan's red-headed stepsister waved excitedly, and Bex's nerves lifted a little.

'Bex, come and meet everyone!' Lorna called, slipping out of her seat to give Bex a quick hug before taking her by the hand, at which point she led her through the pub to a table in the corner, where a man and woman her own age were sitting.

'Bex, this is Eilidh and Niall. Eilidh, Niall, this is Bex, the one I told you about – she's working up at Fergus's. How long did you say you're going to be there for?'

'Well, it was meant to be two months,' Bex said. 'But judging from the amount of work I have to do there, I think I might be here until I'm fifty.'

'Sounds perfect,' Lorna said with a laugh, 'as long as you're a fan of wine.'

'I absolutely am.'

'Then make sure you keep an eye on your glass,' Niall said, stretching out his hand to shake Bex's. 'Eilidh here will take more than her fair share if you let her.'

'That is not true!' Eilidh laughed, rolling her eyes as she punched Niall lightly on the shoulder. 'I'm very fair with my wine.'

'Well, it's either that or you're a complete lightweight,' Niall teased, 'because I swear, no one else gets drunk on two glasses like you do.'

'I do not get that drunk!' Eilidh protested, laughing. 'You're just an excessively slow drinker.'

Bex got the impression that this was the kind of back-and-forth ribbing that could go on for hours, much the same way as with her friends back at home, and despite the fact it had only been a few days since she had said goodbye to Daisy and Claire, she was struck by an unexpected pang of homesickness.

'Come on,' Lorna said, hooking her arm through Bex's. 'I was just about to go to the bar to get more wine. You can help me with the glasses – unless you'd rather have whisky. They've got some pretty good options here.'

'Wine sounds good,' Bex said, following her to the bar.

As they waited to be served, Bex found her attention drawn back to the table, where Niall and Eilidh were laughing and nudging each other.

'So I take it those two are a couple?' she asked.

Lorna's lips pressed together.

'You'd think so, wouldn't you? They're perfect together. But apparently, neither of them is interested.'

Bex watched for another moment as Eilidh reached across and brushed something off Niall's cheek.

'Really?' she said. 'They're not interested in one another? They definitely look interested.'

'I know.' Lorna rolled her eyes as she let out a sigh. 'It's crazy. One day, they'll finally figure it out, get together, and I'll be the only one left single.'

'So you're single too?' Bex asked, surprisingly relieved by this news. Sure, she was used to being the fifth wheel, as the only single one in the group at home, but it got tough sometimes, being the only one to head home alone at night. It would be a change to have someone who understood how that felt.

Lorna nodded. 'Pretty slim pickings around here. The good ones are taken, and the bad ones – well, they come through when they've got a big shoot up at the castle or something, but my days of that kind of flirting are over. I've accepted that it's either move somewhere else or stay here and eventually take over Moira's role as village spinster.'

'Moira?' Bex said, only to follow Lorna's gaze to a woman sitting in the corner with a dram of whisky in front of her and knitting needles in her hands.

'Yup. No one knows how old she actually is.' Lorna laughed. 'My mum reckons she must be in her nineties, but I'm pretty sure no one in their nineties could drink that much and survive. Honestly, you should see her at Burns night. You wouldn't think it to look at her, but that woman can dance. As for her age, I reckon the laird knows, though. He's probably one of the oldest left in the village, after her.'

'Is it laird or lord?' Bex said. It was a question she'd wanted to ask since Fergus had first introduced himself. She hadn't been sure if it had just been his accent, and that didn't seem like something she could say. 'It's been confusing me...'

'Fergus is both. He's a lord – that's his title – but laird's the term we give to landowners here too.'

'So you could be a laird without being a lord, but most lords are also lairds?' Bex asked, wanting to check she had understood fully.

'That's it. Apparently, him and Moira were quite close growing up, but she doesn't go down to the hall much any more unless it's a special occasion. I don't know if it's the walk down there, or if something happened. Then again, one day, we might find out she's only in her fifties and just ages really badly, although I don't think that's likely, because my dad said she was ancient when he was a kid. But you know what it's like when you're little – everyone over eighteen seems ancient.'

Bex studied the woman for a moment or two longer. She looked perfectly content there, clicking away with her needles, occasionally sipping at her drink. As she watched, a young child ran up to her, and Moira stopped her knitting to ruffle the child's hair and hand him a sweet before he disappeared.

Maybe being the old village spinster wouldn't be the worst thing in the world, she thought. Not in a place like this.

'You have to be joking.'

Lorna's voice drew Bex's attention back, and when she looked at her new friend, her jaw was clenched so hard a muscle was twitching in her neck.

'What is it?' Bex asked, unsure what had caused her good mood to change so suddenly.

'Not what,' Lorna said through gritted teeth, 'but who. And the who is Katty McLeod.'

17

Bex was sure she had to have misheard. Katty? Was Katty a name? Maybe Lorna's thick accent was making it hard to understand. She opened her mouth, ready to ask Lorna to repeat herself, but as it turned out, there was no need.

'You heard me right,' Lorna said, continuing to glare at the door. 'Katty McLeod. And trust me, never has a person been more aptly named.'

Bex glanced across at the woman in question. Katty looked to be about their age, with bright blonde hair woven into an intricate braid that fell over her shoulder. She was one of those women who made simple look stylish, in light blue jeans, with a black vest top and a pair of strappy sandals. But despite Lorna knowing who she was, the way Katty's eyes darted around the room as she stood there reminded Bex of herself when she had walked in only a few minutes before. She looked nervous. Unsure if she was in the right place.

'Pretend you haven't seen her,' Lorna hissed, suddenly swivelling back around to face the bar, putting her back to Katty.

'I don't think that's going to work,' Bex whispered back.

'She's heading this way.' And it was more than heading – Katty was striding directly towards Lorna, her eyes locked, as if she had a mission.

'Crap. Crap!' Lorna muttered under her breath.

'Lorna, I was hoping to see you,' Katty said, utterly ignoring Bex. Bex didn't mind; whatever was going on here, she was glad not to be a part of it. Lorna's entire body was tense, a bulging vein visible on her neck.

'Katty,' she said, turning slowly around. 'What an unpleasant surprise this is.'

Katty's smile faltered and her lips twisted tightly together. Bex assumed the woman would hold her ground. Perhaps send a scathing remark back in Lorna's direction, but instead, her face dropped into a deep scowl as a heavy sigh blew from her lips.

'Look, I get it, I messed up. But I need your help. If you could just ask Duncan to listen to my messages – or to sit down and talk to me—'

'Okay, stop right there,' Lorna said, raising her hands in front of her. 'Let's make two things clear. One, you're a grown adult, and I am nobody's messenger. You want to speak to someone, then you speak to him yourself.'

'But he won't—'

'And two,' Lorna continued, cutting Katty off, 'you cheated on my brother. You screwed this up – literally – when you made a not-at-all-metaphorical bed with Archie Campbell. There is nothing you could say to make me help you speak to my brother again. In fact, as far as I'm concerned, his life would be a thousand times better if he never crossed paths with you again. Do I make myself clear?'

Bex felt her breath catch in her lungs and she didn't dare exhale. Katty didn't look like the kind of person who would be happy about being spoken to like that, especially not now that half the pub had gone silent and was staring at them. But Bex didn't need to know Lorna well to sense that she wasn't going to back down. At least now Bex knew that Lorna's warning about Duncan wasn't personal. She had very good reason to want to protect her stepbrother's heart.

With the tension growing tighter and tighter by the second, Bex watched the two women, locked in a silent battle of wills, until finally, Katty flicked her hair back.

'Well, I think I might stay for a drink anyway,' she said, forcing a smile. 'Since I'm here and all.'

'Do whatever you like,' Lorna replied. 'Just do it away from me – and my brother.'

18

Bex had to give it to Katty. That woman had guts. She wasn't sure she'd have had the courage to stay in the pub and have a drink after being spoken to like that. Certainly not when it was clear that every single person had heard the altercation. But with a smile plastered firmly on her face, Katty pushed her shoulders back and marched to the other end of the bar.

'So, that's Duncan's ex-girlfriend?' Bex said quietly to herself. As much as she hated it, she was unable to take her eyes off Katty as she strode away from them. It made sense – she was strikingly beautiful. Bex could easily imagine the pair of them attending a fancy ball at the castle, turning everyone's heads as they strode in arm and arm. Would Duncan wear a kilt to such events? she wondered. He would definitely look good in a kilt, and if he did, did he wear anything underneath?

'Bitch,' Lorna muttered. Bex felt her cheeks flush with heat as for a split second she feared she might have said her thoughts aloud, but with a flutter of relief, she saw that Lorna was glaring down at the end of the bar, all her animosity aimed at Katty.

Pushing thoughts of what may or may not be hidden under Duncan's kilt, Bex cleared her throat.

'So, that's Duncan's ex-girlfriend?' she repeated, this time loud enough for Lorna to hear.

'No, not ex-girlfriend. Ex-fiancée.'

'What?' Bex didn't bother hiding her surprise. 'She was engaged to Duncan – and she cheated on him?'

A slight smile flickered across Lorna's lips, like she knew Bex had been imagining her brother in a kilt.

'It gets worse.'

From the sinking feeling in Bex's stomach, she already suspected why.

'Please don't tell me it was with his best friend,' Bex said.

Lorna grimaced. 'Yup. They'd been best friends since play-group. Tight as a drum. And not just Duncan and Archie, the three of them. Katty too. Course, Duncan and Archie've always been chalk and cheese. Archie's all about making money, bigger houses, flashier cars, you know, that kind of thing. Duncan doesn't care a bit about stuff like that. Everyone knew they both loved her, but no one was surprised when she chose Duncan. He's just... better.' She chuckled lightly at her own remark. 'I know you're probably thinking it's just 'cause I'm his little sister that I'm saying that, but I can tell you there's not a sane woman who would pick that prick Archie over Duncan. But I guess it's true, good guys finish last. Which sucks, because it feels like good women finish last too a lot of the time, and I'm not sure how that's supposed to work.'

There was something in Lorna's wistful tone that made Bex think she was speaking from her own experience as well, but their first drink out didn't seem the time to bring up their own dating histories. Particularly not when Bex was still keen to know more of what had happened with Duncan.

'So I take it she's not with Archie now?' Bex asked, hoping she wasn't coming across as nosy or prying.

'Who knows?' Lorna shrugged. 'She insisted it was a one-time drunken mistake, but we all called bull on that. For starters, when Duncan caught them, it was three in the afternoon. Hardly the time for a drunken slip-up, is it?'

'Duncan caught them?' Bex let out a low whistle. 'Wow. This really is as bad as it gets.'

'I know, right?'

'When did all this happen?' Bex asked. The Duncan she'd met this morning, and again in the study and outside the café, hadn't shown any signs of the heartbreak she would have expected. Then again, she'd had her own heart broken enough times in the past year that no one could tell any more – no one except Claire and Daisy, of course.

'It was about three months ago now,' Lorna told her as she shot another glare in Katty's direction. 'He's always spent most of his time up at the castle as Fergus has always liked having him there, but after it happened, he basically never left. For the first month I had to bring food parcels to the lodge because I was terrified he'd just stop eating.'

'That's terrible,' Bex said, surprised by the level of sympathy she felt for a man she barely knew. While she remained slipped away in her thoughts, Lorna ordered a bottle of wine for the table. Though this was only their second conversation, Bex could feel her fondness for Lorna growing. She could already tell Lorna would be one of those no-bull-type friends that would say things like it was, even if that wasn't what you wanted to hear. No doubt she had told Duncan countless times that he'd be better off without Katty. Probably when she was delivering the food parcels.

Another unexpected twinge of homesickness struck her. She

had a big brother too, and while they were close enough, they weren't that close. They'd ring each other every few months, and he'd stayed at her flat with his girlfriend when they went to a show in London, mostly to save on a hotel. She couldn't imagine bringing him care packages after a breakup. She couldn't even imagine telling him about one of her breakups.

'I should apologise to you,' Lorna said, suddenly breaking Bex's stream of thoughts.

'You should?' Bex asked, surprised.

'Why?'

'For how I reacted this morning.' The barman held out a card machine and Bex reached for her pocket, but Lorna shook her head and immediately tapped hers and paid for the bill before she carried on. 'This morning, seeing him outside with you was one of the first times I've seen him look like himself since it all happened. That's probably why I was a bit harsh, warning you off him and everything. It's just I still have the image of him seared in my mind, you know. After she broke his heart. He was just so down, all the time. No spark at all. None of his trademark grins. He just didn't seem to care about life. It felt like I lost my brother. I'm not sure I could cope with that again.'

'I get it,' Bex said. 'And don't worry, there was nothing going on between me and Duncan at all. We were just talking. The last thing I want to do is add complications to my job. Besides, I doubt I'll have time to even come out that often, with the amount of work there is for me at the castle.'

'You didn't say what it is you're doing exactly,' Lorna said, picking up the bottle of wine and two glasses from the bar, leaving Bex to get the others. 'You can tell us while we get through this. And we can both try to pretend that Eilidh and Niall aren't totally into each other.'

19

Any reservations Bex had about telling Lorna and the others what her role at the castle was had faded; it was clear that everyone in the village knew everyone else's business anyway. She'd rather they heard it from her than have them think she was being all coy and secretive.

'Apparently his wife, Winny, used to do most of the accounts, but I'm guessing she's not around any more?'

'Winny?' Eilidh raised her eyebrows. 'She hasn't been around for almost twenty-five years.'

'What?' Bex nearly spat out the wine she was drinking. The person who had been in charge of the accounts that she now had to sort out had died nearly twenty-five years ago? Who had been doing it since then? Certainly not Fergus. No wonder she had so much of a mess to clear up. It was a miracle he hadn't gone bankrupt. Then again, it was just him in that place and from what she had seen, he didn't have much in the way of expensive taste. Unless you considered dog food, because she doubted the raw meat and tins she had seen in the kitchen came cheap.

'Yup. She passed away when I was in primary school. I remember it,' Eilidh continued. 'We all went to the funeral.'

'I remember,' Niall said. 'We stood next to each other, and you had to share my coat because you insisted you weren't cold.'

'I don't remember that,' Eilidh replied, smiling.

'Oh, I do,' he said, grinning back.

As the old friends continued their trip down memory lane, Bex thought about the implications of what they were telling her. At a guess, she would say that Fergus was around eighty. Meaning he would have been around fifty-five when his wife had died. Fifty-five wasn't that old. Not by today's standards, in any way.

'Has Fergus been on his own this whole time?' she asked. 'Over twenty years?'

'Yup,' Lorna said, taking a sip of her drink. 'I mean, Duncan is the one who knows all the dates. He grew up at the lodge and everything, before our parents married. He would remember Winny's passing better than anyone else. I think he and his dad went in the car with Fergus to the funeral.'

So Bex had been right in thinking that the two of them were very close, but it was the questions about Fergus that were continuing to occupy her thoughts.

'There must have been other women in Fergus's life since then though?' she asked, still not able to drop the subject. 'Has he not had other girlfriends? Did he not think about marrying again?'

'Trust me,' Lorna said, 'he would have no problem. Anyone over the age of fifty still believes he's the most dashing man around, if you can believe that. All because he was super-hot when he was our age, apparently.'

Bex could hardly picture it, but she kept that thought to herself.

'I guess he must have really loved Winny,' she said, trying to imagine what it would be like to choose a lifetime of loneliness than let anyone else into your heart. Would Duncan feel that way, she wondered? If he'd thought Katty was the love of his life – which he obviously had, given that he'd proposed – would he give up on finding anyone else now? No, that didn't seem right – not when he was still so young.

Her eyes involuntarily drifted to Katty, who was still sipping her wine. It hadn't been the first time Bex had found herself inadvertently seeking out the ex-fiancée. For a while, Katty had taken a seat near Moira, but she was now back on her own. From what Bex had seen, not one person had walked over to her and attempted to make conversation, and she couldn't help but think it said a lot about Duncan that the others were giving Katty such a wide berth.

'Oh shit,' Niall said. Bex swivelled around, wondering what had caused his reaction, only to notice the way Lorna's cheeks had paled too.

'This is not good,' Lorna muttered. 'Not good at all.'

At first Bex assumed Lorna was looking back at Katty, but following her gaze, she realised instead that she was staring towards the doorway, now blocked by a figure. A very attractive figure with sandy hair, green-blue eyes and a suspected aroma of pine that unfortunately she couldn't sense from all the way over here, no matter how much she wanted to.

Bex's pulse quickened as she tried to swallow the lump that had forced its way up her throat. She had an inkling that their quiet drink was going to become anything but.

20

'Maybe they won't see each other,' Bex whispered, although from the knot of tension tightening in her stomach and the absolute silence that had fallen over the pub, she knew there was little chance of that. Everyone seemed to know exactly what was going on – except possibly Duncan, who was still standing in the doorway, his gaze sweeping across the room. The moment he spotted Katty, his cheeks tightened, jaw clenched, and tension visibly locked down his neck and shoulders. Bex found it hard to believe he and Lorna were only stepsiblings – they seemed to bristle in the same way.

She was still wondering who was going to be the first to speak when Lorna pushed herself up from her chair, legs stretched out as she rose to her full height. In five brisk strides, she was next to Duncan. 'Please tell me this is a coincidence,' Lorna said, her voice a low hiss, though still just loud enough for those close by to hear. Or maybe it was just that Bex was straining to catch every word, her heart hammering wildly in her chest.

'Of course it's a coincidence,' Duncan replied, his tone light. 'Can't a guy just fancy getting out of the lodge for a bit?'

'Well, then you can sit with us.' Lorna hooked her arm in his and marched him over towards the table, at which point she grabbed a free chair and pushed it in between hers and Bex's. 'Roddy,' she said, waving over to the bar. 'We'll need another glass.'

An uneasy silence settled around them. Bex was desperate to look at Duncan, to see if he was sneaking glances at Katty, but instead, she kept her eyes locked straight ahead. Eilidh and Niall focused on one another, while most people in the pub resumed their conversations – though Bex could feel several curious glances still lingering on them.

'Just so you know, I'm not gatecrashing,' Duncan said, directing his words to Bex. 'Well, I guess I am, but I didn't mean to. I didn't think you guys would be at the White Hart. I assumed you'd be over at the Lion, given that Lorna works there and all.'

'You work in a pub too?' Bex asked her, grateful Duncan hadn't mentioned anything about asking her out for a drink tonight. She wasn't sure the room could cope with any more tension. Or the table, for that matter. Everyone looked as though they were having a hard time focusing as their eyes kept slipping across to where Katty was still perched at the end of the bar. 'You work there as well as the café?'

'And the village shop,' Eilidh said. 'Not to mention the shifts she takes at the hotel. What was it you were doing last time? Chambermaiding? Receptionist? Kitchen porter?'

'A little bit of all of them,' Lorna said as if it was nothing.

'Exactly how many jobs do you have?' Bex said, looking at Lorna with a new sense of awe.

'Too many,' Duncan answered with a playful glare at his sister. 'I keep telling her she needs to slow down and live a little.'

Lorna shrugged. 'But we can't all get a house with a job, can we?' she said, matching his glare with a withering look of her own, before turning back to Bex. 'I've got a lot I want to do. Travel, buy my own place, start my own business. I figure I might as well earn money while I'm young and have got the energy.'

'Really? What kind of business are you thinking of?'

Lorna took a sip of her drink. 'To be honest, I don't know. I just know I don't want to work for other people forever. I want to be able to set my own hours, maybe travel. But that's about all I've got.'

'There must be something you could do,' Bex said, mulling the thought over. Some people were just better at working independently rather than following other people's rules. She had seen that with Daisy. Her best friend had struggled to hold down a job when she lived in London, given that she was always getting itchy feet and an urge to move on. But since she'd started her coffee shop on the canal, she'd never been happier. In fact, she was always talking about what it would be like running it when she and Theo were an old couple, so clearly there was no case of itchy feet there.

'I thought about social media management,' Lorna said. 'But I can't stand being on my phone all day, and I did personal training for a while, but everyone wants early-morning sessions, by which I mean really early. Like 5.30 a.m. I don't mind mornings, but that's just ridiculous. Still, I've got plenty of time. When the right thing comes along, I'll know.'

Bex loved the easy way Lorna spoke about her future. Not to mention the way she seemed so happy to try different things. Bex had known exactly what her career plan was by the time she'd started her A levels, at which point she began checking off milestones as quickly as possible, which started with getting the grades she needed to get her degree. By Lorna's age – she had to be twenty-five or twenty-six – Bex was already managing a team of five, most of whom were older than her, and every career choice she had taken since then had been with the very specific aim of moving another rung higher on the ladder. And that included the bizarre situation she found herself in now.

'So, Bex was just telling us about her new job,' Eilidh said, glancing at Duncan. 'I think we could use someone to sort out our books at the farm.'

'You're not the only one,' Lorna added. While Lorna was still managing to maintain an active role in the conversation, Bex couldn't help but notice the way her gaze continued to flicker back to Katty. 'Irene's bookkeeping at the café causes me to have kittens half the time, but I can't do anything about it – and it's still better than what I see at the Lion, anyway.'

'So, Bex, how have you found your first day here?' Duncan said, looking at her with the slightest smile on his lips. 'Apart from the little mishap this morning, that is.'

'Mishap?' Eilidh said. 'What happened?'

'Nothing,' Bex said hurriedly, feeling a blush creeping up her cheeks. Why the hell would he say something about that in front of everyone? Wasn't he the one who had said he wanted to start over?

Lorna's eyes narrowed suspiciously. 'Oh, come on. You have to spill – it must be juicy, or you wouldn't be trying so hard to keep it quiet.'

A lump had lodged in Bex's throat. She looked at Duncan, hoping he'd say something to ease the speculation, but instead, he tossed his arm over her shoulder and let out a loud laugh. 'Oh, you are just too funny, Bex,' he said, his voice unnaturally cheerful. 'I've really had such a laugh since you got here.'

Bex frowned, about to knock his arm off her shoulder as she

tried to figure out what was going on. That was when she noticed Katty's expression. She was watching them both intently, a deep scowl on her face as her eyes fixed on the way Duncan's arm was draped over Bex. Bex looked back at Duncan, ready to say something, when he laughed again.

'Oh, we're going to have so much fun, aren't we?' he said. 'I can just feel it. Can't you?'

21

With every passing minute, Bex could feel herself getting angrier. Duncan's game was so obvious. Every time Katty glanced in their direction, he would laugh louder than necessary, or shift a little closer to Bex. At one point, he even reached out to brush her hair behind her ear, but she slapped his hand away before he could, not willing to let him get away with that. By the time they'd finished the bottle of wine, she had no desire to stay – not with Duncan there. It was a shame, because she had really liked meeting the others, but the pub had gotten a lot busier, and every time one of them went to the loo, someone would ask if they could take the chair. Leaving would help free up some space for others and so, when her glass was empty, she grabbed her bag and stood up.

'Lorna, thank you so much for inviting me tonight. It's been lovely.'

'You're going already?' Lorna made no attempt to hide her disappointment. 'But you've only had a glass and a half.'

'I know, but any more and I won't be able to get up in the morning. I'd really like to do this again sometime, though?'

'Of course, I'll text you,' Lorna replied, standing up to pull her in for a tight hug, only for Eilidh and Niall to do the same. Though when it came to Duncan, Bex had no intention of hugging him goodbye.

She turned to him and offered a curt nod instead, but as she moved towards the door, he was on his feet. 'I'll walk you back,' he said. 'I was about to leave, anyway.'

'Well, I drove,' Bex said firmly. 'I'm fine.'

'Then I'll walk you to your car.'

'I'm perfectly capable of walking myself to my car.'

'I know that, it's just...' As Duncan's voice faded, his eyes flickered back to Katty, and when his gaze returned to Bex, she saw it all. The desperation, the hurt. The pleading even. Her muscles clenched. She should tell him to do one, she thought. After all, he had made her feel totally uncomfortable. Why shouldn't she make it awkward for him, too? But that wasn't the type of person she was.

'Fine, you can walk me to the car.'

A wave of relief washed over his face. 'I'll be back in a minute, Lorna. Don't let anyone take my chair, and the next round's on me.'

'Fine, I'm holding you to that,' Lorna said, kissing her brother's cheek.

Bex headed outside without bothering to check if he was following; somehow, she could feel his presence just behind her. Whether it was because he was so tall or just intense, she wasn't sure. Whatever spark she'd felt between them that morning had vanished. He'd swung his arm around her shoulder several times tonight, and all she'd done was grimace. Only when she heard the pub door close behind them did she turn around to face him.

'What the hell was that?' she demanded.

As she stood there, glowering at the man who was at least a foot taller than her, she realised she expected him to play innocent, to act as if he didn't know what she was talking about. But instead, his face fell. With a shake of his head, he combed his fingers through his hair.

'I'm really sorry. I am. It's just my ex was there. I wasn't expecting to see her, and I didn't know how to act.'

Her anger faded by a fraction, but it was far from gone.

'Well, that much was obvious,' she said, crossing her arms. 'Just so you know, I was having a really nice night until you came along – and ruined it.'

She hadn't thought he could look any more crestfallen, but the way he bit down on his bottom lip and stared at his feet made her stomach twist with something close to pity.

'I'm sorry. Really, I am. Look, you go back in and I'll head home.'

'No.' Bex shook her head. 'I meant what I said. I need a clear head to work tomorrow. I just hope Lorna has another day off sometime before I leave.'

'She does work bloody hard,' Duncan replied, then quickly realised his misstep. 'I mean, I'm sure she'll have some time off. Absolutely.'

A silence fell between them, but it wasn't like the awkward tension they'd felt sitting around the table. This was different, like there was more they wanted to say but didn't know how.

'Look, Bex,' Duncan said quietly, breaking the silence. 'I really am sorry. I know it's not much, but I did genuinely have a lovely time getting to know you – despite acting like a complete idiot for most of it.' He flashed her one of those smiles, one that quirked ever so slightly at the corner of his lips, and it was clear he was trying to charm his way to her forgiveness, but there was a difference between understanding and accepting what he had done and why, and forgiving him.

'That's an understatement,' she replied.

'So maybe I could make it up to you?' he said, looking down at her with earnest eyes. 'I'd still really like to take you out for a drink, or maybe... dinner?'

As he gazed down with those big blue-green eyes, the corkscrew in her stomach twisted into something warmer. Damn him. Why did he have to be so good-looking and charming? And, apart from tonight's fiasco, he actually seemed like a genuinely nice guy. She'd dated plenty who were far worse than him and who couldn't admit to their mistakes as easily as he just had. But that didn't mean she was going to say yes to him now.

'I think tonight's little performance showed that you are in no position to take any woman out for dinner or drinks yet,' she replied. 'Not when being within ten feet of your ex turns you into an absolute slimeball.'

'Harsh.' He grinned. 'But probably deserved. Just an apology drink then? You have to let me do something to make up for being such an arse.'

Bex contemplated his offer. He really did seem genuinely embarrassed and ashamed by the way he had acted, but that didn't change the fact that he was totally undateable, and she had dated enough undateable men to know.

'Even if I wanted to, I don't have time,' she said, with a sense of finality to her tone. 'If you really want to make it up to me, then help me sort out Fergus's paperwork.'

'I can do that.'

'What?' She looked at his face to find he was being serious. 'I was joking.'

'No, you weren't. I've seen that study. Sorting through all that paperwork is not a one-person job. Plus, it might be helpful to have me there. I know a fair bit about the business. There might be things I can help make sense of for you. Invoices, tenancies. That type of stuff.'

Bex mulled the offer through. There was no denying it might be helpful. Even if all he did was riffle through the papers and bin all Fergus's old Mars bar wrappers, that would be one task she didn't have to do.

'You have a job,' she said, suddenly realising the major flaw in his plan. 'How exactly do you plan on helping me while still doing that?'

'I'll do it in my lunch break. And I'll even bring you your lunch too. For a week.'

Now he had put food on the table it was even harder to say no. Just him bringing her lunch would save a massive amount of time.

'Okay, you have a deal,' she said. 'You can help me for five days. Earn your forgiveness that way.'

'Great.' He grinned, a mischievous glint shining in his eyes. 'Only I've got one condition too.'

'That isn't the way this is working,' Bex said. 'You're the one who needs to make up for being an arse to me, remember?'

He nodded and took a step closer to her. 'I know, and I will. And after five days of helping with paperwork, I want to take you on a date.'

Bex scoffed. 'I'm sorry. Have you forgotten what just happened in there with your ex? I am not going on a date with you. You are in no state to date anyone.'

She saw the hurt flash across his face, but she was telling the truth. There was no point denying it.

'Tonight was a blip, that was all. I just hadn't expected to see her there. And not on today of all days.' Any hint of his cheeky grin had gone. Instead, it looked as though there was a heavy weight pressing down on him.

'Today? Why, what's today?'

Bex watched Duncan's chest rise and fall as he let out a long sigh.

'Today is the anniversary of when I proposed.'

'Crap...' Bex said. The vowel sound stretched out far longer than intended. 'Okay, I get that was pretty tough. Did Lorna not know? She must have known.'

'I think she'll probably realise later,' he said. 'I was hardly going to bring it up. Lorna's been walking on eggshells around me for months. You saw how tense she was tonight. I didn't want to make it even worse. Besides, she would probably have dragged Katty out of the pub by her hair had she realised, and the last thing I wanted was to be responsible for my little sister getting barred.'

From the way he spoke, it was clear he had as much love for his sister as she did for him. It was incredibly endearing. But that really wasn't a good reason to go on a date with a guy, was it? Then again, she had been on dates for worse reasons, and this would come with the bonus of free lunches and paperwork help.

'Fine,' she said. 'Five days of help and I'll go on a date with you.'

His eyes lit up.

'Seriously?'

'Unless you act like an arse again.'

He took another step towards her, his eyes fixed on hers with such intensity, she found herself involuntarily holding her breath.

'Trust me, there's no chance of that happening ever again.'

'Fine then,' she said, before turning to her car and letting the air free from her lungs. 'I'll see you tomorrow. And don't be late.'

22

When Bex finally crawled into bed that night, she found messages waiting from both Claire and Daisy, asking her how the day had gone. How had it gone? There was more work than she'd ever thought possible, and she had a horrible feeling that she was developing a crush on the burly groundskeeper who was in a major rebound phase, and she'd also been warned off by his stepsister, who was now her main friend in the village. That was the truth of it, but if she sent a message like that, she'd spend the next hour and a half fielding their questions, and she didn't have the energy for that. So instead, she sent a basic 'All good; I'll fill you in later' message. She knew she wouldn't get away with that response for long, but it would do for now.

The next morning, as the dawn chorus forced her awake, Bex rolled over in bed, only to find her feet trapped in place. As if someone, or something, was pinning them down.

'What the hell?' she said. Her eyes snapped open as she sat bolt upright, pulse soaring, although as she stared at the end of the bed where her feet were pinned down, she didn't know whether she should laugh or cry.

'Ruby!' The sleeping dog blinked lazily. 'Ruby, what are you doing?' Finally, as Bex prised her feet out from under the dead-weight animal, Ruby lifted her head and gave Bex a quizzical look. 'This is not your bed,' Bex clarified. 'It is not your bed, and I am not your owner. You hear me, right? I am not your person. Fergus is. Go to Fergus. Now!'

Rather than leaping off and hurrying downstairs, the way Bex had expected the animal to do, Ruby simply shuffled farther up the bed, until her head was almost on the pillow next to Bex's head. Her heavy tail thumped against the duvet before she leaned forward and licked Bex along the cheek.

'Urgh!' Bex pushed the dog away and stood up. 'You have horrible morning breath. And I'm not a lick-in-the-morning type of person. Actually, I'm a never-lick-on-the-face type of person. Do you understand? Bad dog, Ruby!'

The moment those two words left Bex's lips, she regretted it. Ruby's face dropped. Her eyes widened and her tail stopped mid-air, as if it couldn't even finish that last half wag. Bizarrely, it reminded Bex of the way Duncan had looked the night before when she told him he'd ruined her night. Although, this time, she felt a lot more guilt. After all, all Ruby had been trying to do was show her a bit of affection.

'I'm sorry,' she said, sitting back down on the bed and rubbing Ruby's head. 'You're not a bad dog. Not really. Apart from the fact that you snuck into my room at night and slept on my bed, which wasn't really what I was expecting. But I know you only did it because you want to be with me, right?' As she finished her question, Ruby's tail offered a single slow wag. 'Okay,' Bex replied, thinking through how to respond. The dog still looked upset, and was it really the worst thing if she wanted to be here with her? 'Maybe you could sleep on the chair instead next time. Would that be okay?' She pointed her finger across

the room to the armchair that Ruby had settled in the first time
Fergus had shown Bex up to the room. 'Chair. Ruby, chair.'

This time, Ruby got the instruction. With her tail wagging,
she jumped up, leapt off the bed and immediately climbed into
the armchair.

'Yes, good dog, good dog,' Bex said, hoping the positive reinforcement would work. 'You can sleep here, okay? You can sleep
here.'

She would probably need to check with Fergus that he didn't
mind, but given how he had left the dog waiting outside the café
the day before, she didn't think it would be an issue. A dog who
wanted to sleep in her bed. Just another thing to add to the list
of things to tell the girls about.

It was only when she was in the shower, paying extra attention on washing her slobbery cheek, that Bex remembered the
key Duncan had given her. Her mind had been so busy whirring
with thoughts of the evening that she'd completely forgotten
about it and spent a second night in the castle without locking
her bedroom door, but now that she had a personal guard dog,
and Duncan was well aware that the space was now occupied, it
didn't seem so much of an issue any more.

As Bex walked down the stairs and made her way into the
kitchen, Ruby remained on her heels. As for where Fergus and
the other dogs were she had no idea. Last night, when she had
come home from the pub, she had heard both music and
snoring drifting from his favoured downstairs room, but she
hadn't wanted to intrude. Now though, as she was trying to bake
some of the frozen croissants Lorna had given her, she was
incredibly keen to find the old man, simply so he could show
her how the hell she was supposed to use this oven.

The contraption was absolutely massive. There were doors
on the front – two metal, one glass – and hot plates on the top,

and so many dials. It would make sense for the dials next to the oven doors to be the ones that turned it on, she decided, but did you really need to turn on the entire oven just to cook two croissants? That felt like a massive waste. She would be better off cooking them all, but croissants weren't known for maintaining their freshness, and the last thing she wanted was to start each day with a stale breakfast.

'Hey, knock knock.'

Bex turned around to find herself face to face with her new friend. 'Lorna? What are you doing here?'

'Well, I was going to visit Duncan, but I thought I'd swing past here and see how you were doing. I wasn't even sure you'd be up, but it looks like I came at the right time. Are you all right?'

'No, this oven is ridiculous. I know Fergus doesn't eat at home, but surely some people cook here? Like when his nephew comes to visit?'

'They do,' Lorna replied. 'Which is why there is another, much more practical oven through here.'

Lorna guided Bex through a narrow galley beside the mammoth fridge into a separate back area of the kitchen, where a tabletop oven sat on top of the counter.

'This place is a labyrinth,' Bex said. 'I didn't even see this part of the kitchen.'

'You should wait until you find the doors in the bookcases.' Lorna grinned.

'You're kidding?'

'Nope.' Lorna's grin widened. 'They're for when the servants had to deliver food to the dining hall or other rooms without traipsing through the entire hall. Duncan used to take me through them all when I was a kid. And speaking of my brother, I'm so sorry about his behaviour last night. He's never normally

like that. Ever. Here, I'll do those for you.' She took the croissants out of Bex's hand and placed them straight on the tray.
'Just so you know, we all had a go at him when he came back in.'

'I'd already given him an earful,' Bex admitted. 'I get it,
though. He obviously felt uncomfortable. With Katty there and
everything and the fact that it was exactly a year since he
proposed.'

'It was what?'

Bex watched the realisation dawn on Lorna's face. She held
her hand up against her forehead and groaned.

'How the hell could I have forgotten that? No wonder he was
so freaked out. Crap, now I've got to go over there and apologise
for being the worst sister ever.'

'There's no chance that's the case,' Bex said, but she could
see how upset Lorna was that she'd missed the reason for
Duncan's odd behaviour. 'I think he was actually grateful you
didn't make any fuss about it.'

With a shake of her head, Lorna let out a sigh.

'Probably,' she said eventually. 'Even so, that was still no
reason to make you uncomfortable.' She shook her head again,
although this time much more vigorously, as if she was trying to
dislodge all thoughts of her brother and the evening before.
When she looked back at Bex, her broad smile was back on her
face. 'Anyway, ignore that. The other reason I came was because
I brought you a little housewarming gift. I realise it's not your
house, and you're not staying here forever, but I thought it
would be nice.'

Lorna reached into her bag and pulled out a large candle.
Embedded in the side was the image of a thistle, the rustic
purple flower that was one of the most well-known Scottish
emblems.

'The thistle's Scottish, even if the candle's not technically traditional,' Lorna said. 'Though Eilidh makes them, and they smell divine.'

Bex took a sniff. 'Wow, you're right. Your friend is seriously talented.'

'Oh, you have no idea. She's the most amazing seamstress too. If we're honest, I think she took all the talent I was supposed to have.'

Bex laughed at the comment. Daisy was a phenomenal painter, and Claire was a pretty fantastic musician, so she knew what it felt like to be the under-talented friend. 'That's really sweet, thank you.'

'You're welcome. Hopefully, we'll manage to meet up for some drinks again in the future, though I'm a bit run off my feet with work at the moment.'

'Yeah, you're not the only one,' Bex said, a heavy sigh freeing from her lungs.

'Is it that bad?' Lorna asked.

'Do you want to see?'

Lorna looked to the oven, where the croissants still required much, much longer to cook, then turned back to Bex and shrugged. 'Why not?'

23

Before Bex took Lorna through to show her the state of the study, there was one more thing she needed to do in the kitchen, and that was to find coffee.

'I just don't understand how he doesn't have something. Just a jar of instant,' she said once she had opened every cupboard in the new section, only to find several cloth napkins and half a dozen mugs – which seemed to have been placed there with the sole purpose of mocking her need for caffeine.

'I think Fergus is more a whisky and water person,' Lorna replied.

'Well, I am very much a coffee person,' Bex said. 'I guess I'll just have to drive up to the village later and get some. Come on, let me show you the chaos I've got to work through.'

Ruby had now taken up a spot in the hallway outside the study, as if she knew that was where Bex was going to be for the rest of the day. After shuffling the dog to the side, Bex opened the door, and Lorna let out a little whistle as she stared at the scene in front of her.

'Wow. I mean, wow. You've got to go through all this?'

'I do. I thought I was just coming up here to deal with the finances, but everything has to be organised before I can even think about doing the accounts. I've no idea how long it's gonna take.'

'Wow, well, I should probably let you get on with it. And go and apologise to Duncan. After I give him another bollocking, that is. Don't forget about the croissants, will you?'

Bex smiled. 'Don't worry. I don't forget about breakfast. Ever. And thank you again for the candle. It was a really lovely gift.'

* * *

It turned out that Bex wasn't the only one who didn't forget about breakfast, and once again, the end of her croissant went to Ruby, although given that she had over-cooked them slightly, she wasn't fussed at all.

'I take back what I said,' Fergus said, poking his head around the doorframe a little later. 'Eight o'clock, and you're already in here. Let me guess, you're planning on clocking off early, then?'

'Clocking off?' Bex laughed, gesturing to the stacks of paperwork, notebooks and general detritus around her. 'With all this? I think I'd be here all night if I'm not careful.'

'Good plan,' he replied without a hint of humour. 'Well, if you need anything, I'll be just next door.'

'Thank you,' she said, turning back to her work, although when she looked up again, Fergus was still in the same position, staring at Ruby.

'Funny thing,' he said, gesturing towards the dog. 'Doesn't normally take to people, that one. Wonder if that's a good sign or bad.'

With that, he turned around and left. He really was a strange old man, with his constant blowing hot and cold, but she guessed that could happen when you lived on your own as long as he had done.

A little while later, the grandfather clocked chimed ten o'clock. Though Bex's stomach was still full from the croissants, a dull throbbing had settled behind her temples and it was more than a little irritating, distracting her from the work she needed to do, not to mention slowing her down considerably. What was even more irritating, though, was that the more she managed to clear in the study, the more she realised there was to do, and it wasn't like she even had access to it all.

'Fergus?' Bex opened one of the windows when she saw Fergus standing out there on the ground with the four remaining dogs. She had been considering going outside to find him, but hadn't wanted to lose all that time. The fact that he had appeared outside the window at the very time she needed him was a godsend.

'Let me guess, you want me to take that dog off your hands,' Fergus said as he trundled towards her.

'What? No, she's fine,' Bex said, glancing at the sleeping dog. 'Although she probably needs a walk.' She knew Labradors were renowned for sleeping a lot, but Ruby had got it down to an art.

'Aye, well, kick her out then. Now, did you want something?'

'Yes.' Bex pointed over to the desk in the centre of the room. 'The bottom two drawers are full of ledgers. But the top drawer appears to be locked. I don't suppose you know where the key is? There're probably some important documents in there. I won't need it for a couple of days, but it would help to have access to everything when I get started on the accounts.'

While Winny's colour-coordinated ledgers left something to be desired, it was clear she had worked hard to try to keep things in order. That meant there was a good chance she had chosen the top, lockable drawer of the desk to place the most important documents in.

Fergus scratched his nose, looking mildly uninterested. 'Aye. Key's probably somewhere. But I don't think there's anything you need in there. Just stuff that's not all that important.'

'Right,' Bex replied, trying not to scoff. 'I don't mean to be funny, but I just found last year's bank statement in the wastepaper basket and an electricity bill wedged under one of the tables to stop it from wobbling. I'm pretty sure there's relevant stuff all over this room.'

'Fine.' Fergus sighed. 'I'll have a look. But mind you, don't go touching anything you don't need to.'

'I won't,' Bex assured him, fully aware she was lying through her teeth. The only way she was going to get through this project was by going through absolutely everything, and if that meant finding old family heirlooms along the way, so be it.

By half past eleven, Bex had finally found a rhythm. She was making piles: one for ledgers, one for bank statements, another for invoices and receipts. She had also found a black bag from the kitchen to shove anything she was certain was rubbish in. There was still masses to go through, but at least she had some sort of system now. Having a system and plenty of work helped distract her from the throbbing pain in her temples. She was going to have to go out and buy some instant coffee. And if she ended up staying here long enough, she might just have to order herself a coffee machine and charge it as an expense. Nigel had told her she could have whatever she needed to get this job done, and what she needed was caffeine.

By some miracle, she was over two-thirds of the way through one of the filing cabinets when Ruby started barking.

'You can't do that. Not with my headache... I'll send you back to Fergus if you're not quiet.'

'So, you have a new friend?' Duncan stood in the doorway. Her breaths shallowed. Somehow, he seemed to have grown ever more attractive overnight. His hair was loose and damp, which accentuated its curl, while he was dressed in tight jeans and wellington boots, which had no right to look as good as they did.

Aware of the silence that was burgeoning between them, she opened her mouth to ask if he'd made any progress on the plumbing when her eyes caught the object in his hand – a familiar white cardboard paper cup.

'Is that... coffee for me?' she asked, eyes widening.

'Double-shot cappuccino,' he said with a grin. 'Full-fat milk, same as yesterday.'

'Oh my God,' she breathed, taking the cup gratefully. 'Have I told you yet that you're the most perfect person?'

24

'I'm pretty sure we had an agreement that was lunch and help with sorting,' Duncan said, 'and considering I'm famished, I'd like to start with the lunch part. Though it doesn't look like there's anywhere to sit here. Why don't we go into the drawing room?'

'The drawing room?'

'The room Fergus likes to sit in,' Duncan clarified. 'Or we could go into the ante library. Or the solar if you want to go upstairs.'

Bex didn't even know that a solar was a type of room, although she made an educated guess that it was probably one that captured a lot of sun.

'How many rooms does this castle have?' she asked, aware that she hadn't yet answered Duncan's question.

'Thirty-six,' he said without a moment's hesitation. 'I counted them when I was a kid. Come on, the drawing room's closest and I'd hate to waste time walking upstairs when you'd rather be putting me to work.'

Bex chuckled as she followed him out of the study. At least

she had given him an accurate first impression of what she was like.

'I'm guessing that as you grew up living here, your parents worked in the castle?' Bex said as she walked beside him.

'My mum did,' he said. 'Before she died.'

'I'm sorry.' For some reason she had assumed that Lorna had become his stepsister because his parents had got divorced. It seemed she had got that wrong.

'Yeah, it was a pretty crappy time,' Duncan said as he opened the door to the drawing room, with Ruby being the first to slip inside. 'Fergus let us stay in the lodge anyway, but then when Dad married Carrie – Lorna's mum – we moved into the village. I could never really settle there, though. It felt too busy. So when I turned sixteen, Fergus suggested I move back into the lodge and start working for him. And I've been here ever since.'

There was a lot for Bex to take in and unpack. The fact that he found the village busy was pretty amusing, although this didn't feel like the time to make a joke about it. But before she could say anything, Duncan had pulled a package from his pocket.

'So, time for lunch?' he said, taking a seat.

She lingered, still not sure if she should say something more about what he'd just told her. After all, moving in by yourself at sixteen must be pretty dramatic, even if your family were all living nearby. But, she decided, if Duncan wanted to tell her more, he would.

'What have you brought me?' Bex said instead as she took a seat on the same sofa, although with a fair gap between them. A gap that was immediately filled by Ruby, who then proceeded to stick her nose in Duncan's pocket.

'Hey, these aren't your treats,' he said, pushing her nose away. 'They're Kenna's. You know that.'

'Kenna?' Bex asked. 'You have your own dog?'

'No, I have a cat. Kenna is my number one girl.' From the smile that beamed on his face, he clearly wasn't joking.

'A cat? I didn't figure you as a cat man.'

His smile quirked. 'Well, I'm sure there's lots about me that you haven't figured out yet, but do you want to talk, or eat?'

She actually wanted to do both. Lots of dates she'd been on the guys had just sat there all night, spouting things about themselves as if the sole purpose of arranging dinner had been so they had a captive audience to listen to them recite their own accolades, most of which were substantially exaggerated – and sometimes completely fabricated. Not that this was a date. Not at all. Duncan was undateable. This was more like work colleagues having lunch together. Although what that lunch was, she wasn't quite sure.

'It's a bridie,' Duncan said as he noticed Bex staring at the package he was unwrapping. 'They're pretty famous around these parts.'

'A bridie?' she asked, eyeing it curiously.

'Yes, and they're delicious. But just in case, I brought sandwiches too. Ham or cheese – you can have whichever one you want.'

'Thank you,' Bex replied with a smile. 'But I guess I should try the bridie first, shouldn't I?'

He handed her the item, which appeared to be some kind of pasty, and took a tentative bite.

'It's really good,' she said, immediately taking another bite.

'Glad you like it.'

'I do. It's delicious.' For a full minute she was silently chewing away. She hadn't realised how hungry she was until now, but with its dense meat filling, this was exactly what she needed. She was almost a third of the way through when she spoke again.

'I can't believe Fergus never cooks here,' she said. 'That massive kitchen's just going to waste.'

'The kitchen gets used. Not a lot, but it's pretty busy in shoot season when his nephew Kieron comes up,' Duncan replied. Though she could have been wrong, Bex was sure she saw a muscle twitch along his jaw as he said the nephew's name.

'Not a fan of this Kieron, then?' Bex asked, raising an eyebrow.

Duncan chuckled, shaking his head.

'Different lifestyles, that's all. His mum – Fergus's sister – is a gem of a woman, but Kieron... Well, let's just say he likes the idea of being a laird far more than any of the responsibilities that come with it. He sees it as a social standing thing, rather than a duty to the folk that live here.'

'And it's not a social standing thing?'

'I dare you to ask Fergus that when he's having to sort out all the roadworks around the village again.' Duncan's smile glinted. He was so charming, it made sense why Lorna had warned her off.

'So, what's your relationship with Fergus?' Bex said, keen to learn more about the situation. 'You obviously know him well if you've got free rein over his house.'

'I guess I'm as close to Fergus as he lets people get,' Duncan said.

'Was it his wife's death that shut him off from everyone?' Bex asked gently. 'I'm guessing that's when he really pulled away.'

Duncan shook his head slowly. 'I don't know. From what my dad said, he was like this even before I knew him. It was a marriage of convenience, so to speak. He was looking to produce an heir, but that didn't happen.'

'A marriage of convenience?' Bex asked, surprised. 'You mean, Fergus is—'

'No, he's not.' Duncan chuckled, shaking his head. 'Not that there'd be anything wrong with it, but no. Fergus was quite the catch back in the day. And then, I guess, something happened. Changed him.'

'You think it was a woman?' Bex asked, her curiosity piqued. 'I'd love to know more.'

Duncan grinned, raising an eyebrow. 'I'd love to see you ask him about it.'

She laughed. 'Not happening. But what about you? How come you're the only one here still working for him full-time? Surely he's got the means to hire a lot more people?'

'Oh, I'm not the only one that works for him,' Duncan said. 'He employs half the village, but he doesn't like them around the house. Take Roddy, for instance.'

'Roddy?'

'He was serving behind the bar last night. He's technically the under-butler, but Fergus only wants him around when Kieron's here or for big events. It's the same with Roddy's dad, Horace. He has an all-round butler-slash-steward's position, but the last thing Fergus wants is to be waited on.'

'So what do they do the rest of the time?'

'Horace has plenty to be getting on with behind the scenes. Maintenance on all the buildings mainly, and Roddy's not workshy either. He'll help me out when I need it. We've got farmers who handle most of the land, so I tend to deal with whatever crops up around here. Anything from fixing windows to tree surgery. Whatever's needed.'

'Jack of all trades, then?'

'You could say that.'

Silence swelled between them and Bex found herself

thinking about that sixteen-year-old boy again, here all on his own. At sixteen she wouldn't have known what to do if her phone ran out of credit. She couldn't have imagined being on her own like that. Just like she couldn't imagine how she would cope finding her fiancé in bed with her best friend.

'I'm sorry about what happened with Katty, too,' she said gently. 'Lorna told me a bit about it. That must've been awful.'

Duncan's gaze shifted away as he chewed on his bottom lip. 'Yeah, it wasn't a highlight of my life, I'll tell you that... But hey, everything happens for a reason, right?'

'Do you believe that?' Bex asked.

He looked back at her, his gaze softening.

'Not always. You can't exactly tell a six-year-old who's lost his mum that everything happens for a reason. I know that. But I think it matters what we do after. We just have to make the best of what life throws our way.'

Bex wasn't sure when it had happened, but he was closer than she'd realised. She'd still have to lean forward a fraction to kiss him, though.

With a spike in her pulse, Bex jumped up, shifting a full foot away from the sofa, and tried to swallow, though her throat had turned inexplicably dry. Why was she thinking about kissing him? Maybe it was because of the way he was looking at her, even now. With that same brooding intensity.

'Och, there you are!'

Bex spun around with her heart pounding. Fergus was standing there with the dogs at his side.

'Been looking for you, Duncan. Got old Gregory McLean on the phone – he says his sheep got out. I need some help. I said you'd go down there. Unless I'm interrupting something, of course.'

Fergus's lips twitched.

'No, not at all,' Bex said quickly, trying to compose herself.

'Right. Good. Well, we should get going. Don't want them sheep causing a ruckus.'

'Right.' Duncan looked back at Bex, as if he was going to say something, but instead he reached his hand down and ruffled Ruby's fur. 'I guess I better get off then,' he said. 'Until tomorrow, Rebecca Barker. Ruby.' A moment later, he was gone and Bex was left holding a half-eaten bridie, wondering why her heart was still beating so fast.

25

Fergus's unexpected interruption meant Duncan left before sorting out a single piece of paper and so the next day, when he arrived at lunchtime, with both coffee and sandwiches, Bex put him straight to work.

'And just so you know, yesterday does not count,' she said. 'You had to be helping me, remember? Five days' help and then a drink.'

'I think we said five days' work and then a date, actually,' Duncan replied.

'Let's just see if you can manage five days first,' she said.

His primary role that afternoon was sorting out rubbish – taking the bags she had already filled outside so that she didn't have to waste time walking up and down the hallways. Not to mention using the hoover on some of the more densely cobwebbed corners and bookshelves that Bex hadn't yet started on for fear of what might crawl out from them.

Yet despite the grimness of the work, they laughed and joked, talking about inconsequential matters, such as London traffic and the fact that sheep were allowed to hog the road up here. When he'd left, after they'd spent an hour sorting together, then eaten lunch, Bex was surprised by how keenly she felt his absence. And when the next day, Thursday, rolled around, she found herself glancing at the clock, waiting for the moment Duncan would stride through the study doors, holding coffee in his hands. Annoyingly, it didn't happen.

Instead, at 1 p.m. there was a timid knock on the door and a young man Bex recognised from behind the bar at the White Hart appeared.

'Hi, Bex, right? Duncan asked me to give you these,' he said, lifting his hands to show the coffee and a brown paper bag he was holding. 'And to say sorry. He got stuck doing work.'

'Roddy, isn't it?' she said. He nodded. 'Are you going to see Duncan now?'

'Nah, he's had to go off to fix some fences on the other side of the loch. I need to get to the pub. I had to nip out on my shift. Duncan can be pretty forceful when he wants something doing and I guess he didn't want you to go hungry.'

There was no denying Bex was hungry, but while she was grateful for the food, she was surprised how saddened she was not to be seeing Duncan again.

'Thanks, Roddy, I appreciate it,' she said, taking the food and drink from him, yet as he turned to leave, she spoke again. 'Roddy, I'm guessing if Duncan messaged you to do this, then you've got his phone number, right?'

'Aye, do you want it?'

Bex felt the smile rise on her cheeks.

'Yes please. That would be great.'

* * *

Now that she'd cleared a little more space, Bex sat in the study to eat her lunch and composed her message.

> Five working days. At this rate, that should be about a month and a half until you take me for a drink.

After hitting send on the message, she tucked into her sandwich and watched as the coloured ticks appeared beneath her text. He had read it then.

> It's a date. Not a drink. And I'm just trying to build up the suspense.

She laughed before taking her time to figure out how to respond.

> It's okay, you can admit it. All the heavy lifting of the paper was too much for you.

> Oh, you have no idea how good I am at heavy lifting. But I can show you if you'd like.

Bex cursed herself. What was she doing? It was the most blatant flirting possible, and she had promised both herself and Lorna that she would do nothing of the sort. But it was just a bit of texting, that was all. A bit of fun, and it wasn't like it was going to go anywhere. Which was exactly what she said on the phone to the girls that night.

'He's in the rebound zone,' she said. 'A hundred per cent no go.'

She had merely mentioned how Duncan had helped her the day before, and Daisy and Claire had started squealing like teenagers. 'And clearly unreliable, given that he's only actually helped me once this week.'

'But he had someone bring you your lunch. That's so cute,' Daisy replied.

'Any chance we can get a photo?' Claire said. 'Or at least a surname so I can Facebook stalk him to see what he looks like.'

'I don't think Duncan's the type of person who would even know what a social media profile is,' Bex said. Only then did she realise she'd never seen him with a phone in his hands or even poking out of his pocket. He obviously had one, because they were messaging, but something told her he was the type of guy who had a phone for necessity – or flirting – rather than all the apps and other tools available on it.

'What are you going to do for the rest of the week?' Daisy asked, interrupting Bex's stream of thought.

'Work,' Bex replied. 'There's so much here to sort, there's not much time for anything else. Maybe next week I might actually be able to start looking at the accounts.' Daisy's throat cleared, but before she could get a word in, Bex continued. 'And don't you dare talk to me about working too much when you have that café of yours open every hour of the day. I'm just going to do a bit, that's all.'

There was a slight pause, during which Bex was sure she heard a huff rattle down the line, but she didn't respond.

'Fine, just take care of yourself, that's all. We know you have work to do. But you don't want to overdo it.'

'Daisy's right,' Claire joined in. 'Maybe you can ask Duncan if he knows a good place to help you unwind.'

'Or even better, maybe he can help you unwind,' Daisy added.

Once again, the giggling started and as much as she didn't want to, Bex couldn't help but laugh.

'You two are ridiculous,' she said. 'But I love you very much. Speak soon.'

'Always,' Daisy replied. 'Love you too. And maybe give this Duncan a chance. He sounds like a good one.'

'Yeah, I think he probably is,' Bex said, although the words caused a strange sinking in her stomach. She couldn't help but feel that that was half the problem.

26

On Friday morning, Fergus popped into the study. Ruby had spent the previous few nights sleeping up in Bex's room, on the armchair, and she wondered if he was going to mention it, but instead, he simply scanned the area.

'Looks like you've sorted out a fair bit in here. Maybe you won't be here as long as we thought.'

'This is just tidying, Fergus,' Bex replied. She didn't mean to sound so short, but once again the birds had had her up at an insane hour, and the fact that Fergus seemed completely oblivious to the task he had set her was more than a little irritating. 'I haven't even started on the accounting.'

'Aye, of course,' he mumbled. 'Oh, I found some keys for you. Not sure which opens which, and like I said – if there's stuff that dinnae concern you, just leave it. Nae need to fash yourself about anything that's not money.'

Bex had a long way to go before she understood all the Scottish words that Fergus interjected into their conversations, but she could always gather the meaning.

'Don't worry, I'm leaving anything that's personal aside,' she said, although she wasn't sure why he felt the need to reinforce the point. She was, after all, an accountant. She'd already piled a corner high with artwork, birthday cards and memorabilia that had nothing to do with accounts. Despite his craving for solitude, it was clear Fergus had been well-loved.

'There are some other things in there,' she said, pointing at the pile. 'Maybe you want to take them into the drawing room and go through them?' The old man crinkled his nose as he looked towards the items with something close to a sense of fear.

'They're fine here for now,' he said. 'And I best be getting on. Things to do.'

Bex smiled at the response. She too had things to be getting on with and as useful as it was to have the keys, she had been partway through sorting out a stack of receipts and really wanted to get back to them, but rather than going, Fergus was continuing to linger in the doorway.

'Noticed the lad Duncan seems to have taken a shine to you,' he said. His tone was stoically even, as if he had needed to work to make it sound less pointed. Bex wasn't quite sure why it made her feel so uncomfortable.

'He seems nice,' she said, not sure what else she could add that didn't sound incriminating.

'Aye, he is. Heart of gold, that one. Just like… just like his mother. You best not be playing some games, though. Boy's had enough of that.'

Bex bit down on the inside of her cheek. How the hell was this what her job entailed? She was a senior accountant. One of the most respected members at her firm, and now she was going through papers, fishing out chocolate bar wrappers and being given very unsolicited advice about who she could spend her time with. Not that she and Duncan were even spending that much time together.

'I know about Duncan's situation,' she said. 'And I also know that I am here to do a job, and getting that job done as effectively and efficiently as possible so I can return home to my life in London is my only goal here. Now, as you said, you have things to do. As do I, so you should probably go and do yours and leave me to get on with mine. Don't you think?'

27

The conversation with Fergus left Bex in a foul mood for a multitude of reasons and not just because the only coffee she had had that day had been a very weak instant that she'd picked up at the village shop which did nothing to curb her caffeine needs.

The first reason she was angry was because he'd had the audacity to tell her not to play games with Duncan when he knew absolutely nothing about her. Nothing at all. And if he had known anything about the situation, he would have known that Duncan was the one who had played games with her – or at least tried to use her to make his ex jealous. He was the one actively pursuing her, and she was being the professional. Which led to the second reason she was so angry.

She was a professional. A highly skilled, highly educated woman, and yet he was treating her like what? A cleaner? That was what it felt like. Her brain was desperate for numbers. She was missing her friends, and it was clear that this job was far bigger than he had let on to Nigel, and she was just supposed to act okay with it all.

She was so angry, all morning the blood was whirring behind her ears, and she took to slamming the ledgers down on the piles one after another, with any delicate touch gone. Every drawer she opened with a sharp tug and every cupboard she slammed closed. So much so that more than one rattled on its hinges. That made her cool her touch just a fraction, because the last thing she needed to add to all this was the pain of shattered glass to clear up too. Still, she was busy kicking the side of a filing cabinet because the bottom drawer wouldn't open when a voice made her jump.

'You okay?'

That lilting tone from the doorway caused her stomach to both simultaneously flip and sink. Of course Duncan would choose today to reappear at lunch, just as Fergus had given her the unsubtle warning to keep away.

'Not really,' she said truthfully. 'I'm pissed off.'

'With?'

'With all this,' she said. She waved her hands in the air, indicating the entirety of the study at the same time as driving her toe into the bottom of the jammed filing cabinet drawer. It was stupid – for the last four days she had worked solidly on trying to clear this space, but on the face of it, it was still a disaster. 'All of this.'

In the corner of the room, Ruby let out a light whine before moving across to Bex and nuzzling against her knee.

'Well, obviously, I'm not pissed off at you, girl,' she said, rubbing the dog's ears. 'But I won't lie. It would be helpful if you could help me sort some of this stuff out.'

She didn't realise that Duncan had moved until she felt him beside her, his hand slipping into hers. An unwanted tingle spread through her palm.

'Come on, you'll get through it. I might not know you well,

but I sure as hell know you're not going to let a load of paper beat you. Besides, I'm free this afternoon. I can help you for the rest of the day.'

'You can?' she asked, aware of just how high her voice hitched when she spoke.

'Yes. Actually, I'd like to. It's a darn sight cooler in here. Now tell me, where do you want me to start?'

It was a difficult question to answer. All the obvious pieces of rubbish had already been binned – now everything had to be checked thoroughly to see if it was some sort of statement, bill, or receipt, or just a takeaway leaflet. She let out a long sigh when her eyes fell on the coffee in Duncan's hand. She'd already had two cups today, but the instant granules weren't anywhere near as good or as strong as she needed right now.

'Well, you can start by handing me that coffee,' she said, at which point she took it from him and practically inhaled a third of the cup in one go. 'And this only counts as one day of helping me, got it?'

'You're really going to make me work for that date, aren't you, Barker?'

'Yes,' Bex said. 'I am. And it's a drink, remember. It is not a date.'

28

'That's an invoice from one of the gamekeepers,' Duncan said, picking a piece of paper out of the 'binned' pile where Bex had put it only a moment before.

'How do you know?' Bex asked, squinting. 'There's nothing written on it that says that. It's just a couple of numbers.'

'There.' Duncan pointed to a scrawl at the bottom of the page. 'That's Turlough's signature.'

'God, I thought someone was just trying to make a pen work,' Bex said, grimacing at her mistake, before picking up the rest of the scraps she had placed in the bin pile. 'In that case, maybe you could go through these as well.'

They were an efficient team. Impressively so. With all the obvious rubbish sorted, they were now riffling through the rest. After the first two hours, they had all the ledgers stacked together in one corner of the room, though Bex hadn't dared open any of them. If she did, those tears of pure frustration which had been teetering on the edge of release all morning might well appear, and there was no chance she was going to let that happen.

'Duncan, I've found a couple of handwritten notes here,' she said. She was crouched at the bottom of a bookshelf, which housed dozens of meaty tomes on farming. Though trapped between them had been a small stack of papers. 'They look to be legal things. I don't think it's money, but I'm not sure. It's got information about hospitals on it? Correspondence from them to Fergus, I think. Do we already have a pile for legal stuff?'

Duncan's face pinched. 'Hospitals, you say? That's weird. I found a notebook in here with a list in it. I wasn't sure what they were, but come to think of it, they might have been hospitals too.'

'Can I see?' Bex asked.

'Sure.'

He handed her the small leather notebook, open on the first page. There was a long list of names, all of which had been struck through with a single line, leaving them perfectly legible.

'Edinburgh Royal, Queen Charlotte, Maryfield.' Bex read the first few aloud, although the list went on. While she didn't recognise all of them, she agreed with Duncan that they could well be hospitals. 'Let's put this together with the letters I found. There's a ton of legal ones too. They can go in the same pile. That way, Fergus will know they're all together. Not that I expect him to look through any of it.'

It would be helpful if he would though, she thought. Some of the ones that were full of legal jargon may well be to do with loans or invoices, in which case she would need to come back to them later. So maybe it was better if she put those in a pile of their own.

Her thoughts about the old man continually switched between feeling sorry for him – he was obviously incredibly lonely, after all – and being angry and frustrated. He had access to the type of funds most people could never dream of. There was really no excuse for letting his accounts get into this type of state. Just like there was no excuse for the way he had spoken to her about Duncan when he had no idea of the situation. If he was going to be mad at her for anything, it should be the fact that Ruby very much preferred her to him. That she would understand.

With her thoughts on Fergus, she remembered the jumble of keys he had given her earlier in the day.

'Can you see if you can unlock the desk drawers?' she said to Duncan. 'I'm pretty sure there's some stuff I need access to in there, but I think Fergus'd be happier if you went through them rather than me.'

'Sure,' Duncan said.

Bex held out the keys for him. Yet as Duncan moved to take them from her, his fingertips brushed against her palm. An electric tingle shot out from the place he touched her, and a rush of heat flooded the rest of her body. The tiniest of gasps escaped her lips before she stumbled back, trying to make sense of what had just happened. It was just like the first time they had touched.

Why the hell was her heart beating so damn fast from just touching him? Surely that wasn't normal? And why the hell was he standing there, staring at her with those swimmable blue-green eyes?

'Um, it's that desk,' she said, pointing across the study and trying to act like her pulse hadn't suddenly rocketed.

'You mean the only desk in the room?' Duncan said, the slightest smirk twisting the corners of his lips.

'Yes, that's the one,' she said.

Aware that her cheeks were now fluorescent, Bex turned around and busied herself with a pile of paper she had already sorted. Yet even with her back to him, she could feel Duncan's eyes boring into her. She could sense that slanted smirk on one side of his face too, and it was sending her stomach into a full Cirque du Soleil routine.

It was just because she had been told to steer clear, she told herself. That was the reason she was feeling like this. And it would pass soon enough. She just had to get to know him more. Most of the men she thought were attractive suddenly became less so when she got to know them. That would happen with Duncan too. She was sure of it.

As she finally put down the stack of already sorted paper, Duncan got to work on the desk. After a few minutes of fiddling, he spoke again.

'Got one,' he said. 'And it looks like these might actually be useful to you,' he added, holding out yet another stack of leather-bound ledgers.

'I knew there would be stuff in there I needed,' Bex said, careful not to touch Duncan's hand this time as she took the pile from him.

Despite her desire to leave all the accounts until after the physical sorting had been done, Bex couldn't help flipping through the top ledger. Her eyes lit up. Unlike most of the paper-work she had looked through before, these were surprisingly organised. Blue, black and red ink only, all within the columns, clearly labelled and not the slightest hint of purple anywhere. She was actually feeling rather happy – until she noticed the date on the top. Her jaw dropped.

'These are from fifty years ago?' she exclaimed. 'I can't possibly have to look at the accounts from fifty years ago!'

She wanted to cry. She was going to have to speak to Nigel about this. This was not a one-person job. An entire team had been called in to settle smaller tasks. What he was asking of her was ridiculous, and she was about to say as much to Duncan when he spoke again.

'Oh wow,' he said.

'What is it? Because if you tell me it's a hundred-year-old ledger, then that's it. I'm walking.'

He let out a dry chuckle, but his eyes remained on the items in his hand.

'No, it's not that. I just opened the top drawer and it's mostly old photos and cards,' he said, pulling out a few faded images. 'But this one... My grandad used to have a photo just like this in the house, though I didn't find it until after he'd died. It was locked away in a drawer, a little like this.'

He held it out to her.

It was of two young men and a woman standing between them. From the hint of scenery in the background, it was probably taken somewhere in the grounds, with a view of the loch in the distance. It was the type of photo where you could feel the joy radiating from the paper. All three of them were laughing, with heads thrown back and grins so wide their eyes were creased to almost nothing.

Bex squinted. 'Is that your grandad?' she asked, pointing to the man on the left. Even with the difference in clothes and the angle he stood at, there was a vague resemblance between the man and Duncan, that came mostly from the height.

'Aye, that's my grandad,' Duncan said. 'And that's Fergus.'

'Fergus? As in this Fergus? Grumpy old Laird Fergus?'

Duncan laughed.

'That's the one.'

Bex could hardly believe it. Fergus had once been as dashing as people claimed. In the photo, he wore a flat cap perched jauntily, his wax jacket was clean, and one of his hands was casually in his pocket. With his smile wide and carefree, Bex could barely recognise him.

'So your grandad and Fergus were friends,' Bex said, continuing to study the photograph.

'Apparently, they were very close growing up,' Duncan said. 'Grandad was the groundskeeper here until the day he died, but by that time, he and Fergus hadn't been speaking for years.'

'What? Why? What happened?' Bex said. This insight into the laird's past was substantially more intriguing than all the work that awaited her.

But rather than replying immediately, Duncan let out a long sigh.

'I'm not sure,' he said. 'But something did.'

'Yet your grandad carried on working here? For Fergus? Living in the lodge?'

'I think Fergus knew that no one could do the job better than Grandad, and Grandad knew he'd never find a job he loved more than this. And he didn't want to uproot Mum. That was another crazy relationship. Apparently no one even knew Grandad was seeing anyone, then he turned up with this young woman and announced that she'd had his baby and they were a family now. Well, it wasn't a family that lasted long. She left when Mum was only two, leaving Grandad to be Mum's sole parent. Didn't even stay in touch. I think that's part of why Fergus let them stay. You know, she'd already had a lot of change to deal with.'

'Wow.'

Bex knew lots of families had complications, but her heart went out to Duncan's grandfather. To have lost his best friend and then for his wife to walk out and leave him with a toddler must have been one hell of a lot to deal with.

'Who's the girl?' Bex asked, looking at the third person in the photo. Fergus had his arm slung around the woman's shoulder, while Duncan's grandfather had his hand around her waist.

'No idea,' Duncan said, frowning.

'Do you think maybe she's the reason they fell out?' Bex was weaving a story in her head, with these three people as the main characters. 'Maybe they were both in love with her?'

She could see it now, the beautiful young woman, torn between the dashing laird and the good-hearted groundskeeper. It was the type of story novels were based on.

'I guess it's possible,' Duncan replied quietly.

'Aren't you interested in knowing more?'

'Not really.'

It took Bex a mere heartbeat to realise why Duncan's voice had taken on a distant quality. The instant it did, guilt stirred through her.

Two childhood best friends, torn apart because they loved the same woman. The story she had described was pretty much exactly what had happened with Duncan, Archie and Katty. And yet here she was talking about it like it would be a fun, exciting piece of gossip. Silence swilled around the room. Bex found herself desperate to reach out and take Duncan's hand. To apologise for her thoughtlessness. And yet she suspected he would hate that. Hate her feeling sorry for him.

'Come on,' she said, attempting to break the tension. 'Let's set those aside in case Fergus wants them later. We've got plenty to get through. Unless you're already tired from moving books and need a rest?'

He lifted his gaze and quirked an eyebrow at her.

'Don't worry about me. I've got enough stamina for days. I'll show you if you like.'

'Perfect,' she replied, unable to grin back. 'Because I need that filing cabinet open next.'

29

When they finally finished, it wasn't because they had run out of work to do, but because Ruby was standing at the closed door, scratching to go out.

'What time is it?' Bex asked, having left her phone somewhere in the detritus.

'Um, six,' Duncan replied as he looked at his watch. 'I guess she must be ready for her dinner.'

'Six?' Bex grabbed Duncan's wrist so she could turn his watch around to face her. 'Where the heck did the last three hours go?'

'Well, you know what they say about time flying when you're having fun.' Duncan grinned. 'I guess it must be the company.'

'Yeah,' Bex said in a very noncommittal way. Not that she hadn't enjoyed Duncan's company, but at some point in the last three hours, they had pretty much stopped talking and just got on with work. Now, as she stepped back, she was incredibly grateful for that.

'This actually looks like we've made progress,' she said,

surprise raising her voice. 'This is great. Thank you so much. I don't think I would have been able to do this without your help.'

'Well, how about I get to take you out for that meal now? I mean, if you don't need my help with any more sorting.'

Bex offered him a withering glare.

'I said we've made progress, not that we were done. There's still that extra cupboard at the end that I haven't opened since the first day because I'm pretty sure there are mice living in there.'

Duncan let out a chuckle. 'Well, I can do that one for you then. But I ought to go back now. Kenna hates it when I'm out all day. I've tried to have her come to work with me, you know, just hang around in the truck while I go off and do things, but she doesn't like doing that either.'

'Kenna the cat?' Bex replied. 'You wanted to take your cat to work with you?'

'Why not?' he said, looking most put out by the comment. 'People take dogs to work with them. Why should it be any different?'

Bex couldn't help but study this bulk of a man in front of her. On the outside, he looked like he should spend his days chopping wood and carrying full logs on his shoulders – which he may well do – but there was this other side to him. The side that had looked after himself since he was young, wasn't ashamed for anyone to know how much he loved his sister and his cat, and would spend hours of his afternoon helping a woman he didn't even know. Although, there was a small part of her that suspected the help he had given her wasn't just to do with going for a drink, but also for Fergus. Helping out this old man who'd had such a tempestuous relationship with his grandfather that they'd stopped speaking altogether. It was a strange dynamic, that was for sure.

'Talking of which, Ruby really seems to have taken a liking to you,' Duncan carried on. 'It's strange. She's normally quite aloof with people she doesn't know.'

'Fergus said the same, but I think she just likes the fact that if she hangs out with me, it means she doesn't have to go out walking all day with Fergus.'

Duncan gave a laugh, one so full-bellied and warm that Bex couldn't help but feel her cheeks rise in response.

'Aye, you might be right about that,' he replied. 'Now, it's Friday night. What are your plans? A drink at the White Hart? Dinner at the Lion?'

She laughed. 'You don't give up, do you? And no, my plans are a cheese omelette, an early night, a catch-up with my friends on the phone, and hopefully, if I don't get woken up by the damn birds, a lie-in in the morning.'

A frown formed, crinkling his otherwise creaseless face.

'You're having trouble sleeping here?' he asked, his voice laced with genuine concern.

'Sleeping, no,' Bex replied. 'Staying asleep, yes. Had I known how early these damn birds wake up in summer, I think I would have asked my boss to send me here in winter.' She let out a chuckle, to which Duncan replied with a smile, although it was notably more distant than normal. A second later, his expression cleared.

'Well, like I said, I need to get back to Kenna. I'm sure I'll see you over the weekend, but if I don't,' he said, 'I'll see you on Monday. Only two days left until we go on our date.'

'Um, no,' Bex said, placing her hands on her hips. 'It's three. You have to help me for five days, remember?'

He grinned. 'Oh, I remember what you said. I just think that after two more lunches with me, you'll be the one asking me out on a date instead.'

With that, he flashed her a smile bright enough to light the whole damn castle before offering Ruby one quick stroke, then he opened the door through which both of them disappeared.

30

'You clearly like him,' Daisy said on the phone that night. 'Half the dates you go on don't even make it to the hour point. You were with him most of the day.'

'Yes, because he was useful,' Bex countered. 'And I told you most of the time we weren't even talking, we were just working. Besides, I like Lorna too much to do anything. I don't think she'd forgive me.'

Bex had received a couple of messages from Lorna since she'd dropped in, mainly apologising for being so busy and also saying that she had the following Friday night off and would be meeting up with the others if Bex wanted to join them. Immediately she had sent a reply saying she would be there. The question she wasn't sure about was whether or not she wanted Duncan to be there too.

'Just... make sure you're being sensible,' Daisy said.

'Sensible? What's that supposed to mean?'

'I mean, protect your heart, okay? He's lived up there his whole life, and he's probably got no intention of leaving. I just don't want you getting hurt.'

'Did you not just hear me say I'm steering clear?' Bex said.

'Oh, I heard you, but I also know how the ones you're supposed to steer clear of are the ones you find yourself wanting to spend more time with.'

Bex hummed in annoyance, although she didn't outright disagree. It wasn't an intentional thing to go after the wrong type of men; notorious players who were certain to string her along and break her heart when they got bored. She already knew Duncan wasn't the string-along type. He was the propose-to-your-childhood-sweetheart type. A guy who could show that type of commitment was a far cry from the ones she should have steered clear of in the past.

'Don't worry,' Bex replied. 'I know exactly what I'm walking into. He's a rebound, 100 per cent, and I'm not getting dragged into it. But he's good company, and it's nice to have someone to talk to, especially with the amount of work I have to get through right now.'

'Hopefully it will get better, now you're on the actual accounting part,' Claire said. 'You know, the part you like.'

'Hmm.' It was Bex's second noncommittal hum in as many minutes, but she suspected that the entire job was going to be one uphill battle. A very steep climb, with a well-deserved promotion at the top of it.

'All right, well, let's catch up again over the weekend,' Daisy said. 'Maybe Sunday evening?'

'Perfect,' Bex agreed. 'Love you both.'

'Love you too.'

With a long sigh, Bex dropped her phone down onto the bed, then flopped down beside it. Fingers crossed tomorrow would be so cloudy that the birds didn't even notice it was morning and would let her sleep in until midday. She could always hope.

* * *

'Why are you so loud?' Bex screamed into the pillow as she wrapped it around her ears, trying to block out the noise. Unfortunately, Ruby took the fact that she was now awake as a sign she could jump from her armchair onto the bed. After bouncing her way up the mattress, she flopped next to Bex, her head on the neighbouring pillow, which, Bex had learned, was her favourite position to be in.

For several minutes, Bex kept the pillow over her head and squeezed her eyes shut, trying to block out the noise of the birds and ignore the smell of dog breath that filled her nose. But it was no good. These damn animals weren't going to let her sleep. And if she wasn't sleeping, she might as well get to work.

It was with a flutter of excitement that Bex walked into the study with her laptop. It was the first time she had seen any reason to bring the computer down from her room, and there was still a long way until things were sorted, but at least she could now start digitising what she had, and after the week of sorting, this felt like an absolute treat. With a cup of painfully weak instant coffee at her side, she tried to work out where to start. Bank statements, she decided. That was going to be the best place, and not only that, but she was going to put on some music, too.

Bex had always been one of those people who liked to listen to music while she worked. If she'd had her way, she would have had her speakers on full, blasting upbeat tunes into the entire office, lifting the mood and her work rate every day. But other people didn't feel the same, and so most of the time she resorted to keeping one earbud in so she could enjoy her music, while still being able to hear if anyone needed her. But given that she was working alone, she turned the volume on her computer up to full and felt the smile rise to her lips.

'Why have I not been doing this all week?' she said to Ruby, who looked somewhat perturbed by the strange noises that filled their normally quiet space. 'This is much better, isn't it, girl?'

The Labrador responded with a beat of her tail against the floor, which Bex took as a definite yes. Soon she was so absorbed in placing all the paper bank statements she had into chronological order that she didn't even hear the door open.

'You have to be joking. I knew this would happen.'

Bex turned around to find Duncan standing in the doorway, combing his hands through his hair. 'You're a complete workaholic. You are aware it's Saturday, right?'

Bex hadn't expected to see Duncan, though why she wasn't sure. She didn't know much about being a groundskeeper, but it didn't seem like a job that was confined to normal office hours. Not that she could remember what those were any more.

'Exactly, it's the weekend, which means I have even more hours to work,' Bex replied, though she couldn't hide the small smile tugging at her lips at the sight of him in a plaid shirt. He really wasn't helping her daydreams of him chopping wood like it was some pine-scented aftershave advert. 'So, did you want something, or just to interrupt me?'

'Actually, I came to give you something.'

'Two gifts in one week?' she teased. Though the key had been more of a necessity than a gift, it was still thoughtful. And in her experience, the only time men gave her presents was when they wanted to get her into bed, which she'd made very clear was not going to happen with Duncan.

'I think you might like this one, even more than the key,' he said.

'Well, now I'm intrigued.'

Wordlessly, he slipped his hand into his pocket and pulled out a brown paper bag. The item inside couldn't have been larger than a deck of cards or a pack of cigarettes. As he handed it to her, Bex found herself tempted to brush against his skin again, just to see if she got that same electric feeling. But why would she want to do something like that? Even if he had felt the same spark as she had, it wasn't as if they were going to do anything about it. So instead, she carefully took the bag, opened it up and looked inside.

A loud laugh cracked from her lungs.

'Oh my goodness! Earplugs! You saint.'

The plastic box inside contained five pairs of bright orange foam earplugs, which, according to the label on the outside, had a reduction of 38 decibels. She had no idea whether that was good or not, but it sounded like it should be.

'Thank you,' she said, her eyes meeting Duncan's for the first time all morning. 'This is really thoughtful of you.'

'I'm a thoughtful kind of guy,' he said. 'Speaking of which...'

He turned around and headed back out through the door, before returning a moment later with a far larger box in his hand.

'Oh my God, it's a coffee machine! Is this for me?'

Bex shook her head in disbelief. She'd been considering ordering one herself and charging it to Nigel. She'd probably even mentioned as much to Duncan during one of their conversations.

'Of course it's for you,' he replied. 'Do you know how much takeaway coffees cost? I thought I was going to go broke. So I found a solution.'

He placed the box down on the now-cleared section of the desk.

'We need to get mugs now,' Bex said, excitement sparking in her voice. 'You're staying for one, right?'

Even sorting bank statements and starting on the accounts wasn't as exciting as the thought of constant access to decent coffee. And given that he was the one who had brought her the machine, not to mention the earplugs, the least she could do was offer Duncan a drink, but as he leaned against the door-frame, his smile was broad, and his trademark smirk twisted at the corner of his lips.

'Well, given that it's Saturday, and you really shouldn't be working, I had a different idea for how you could say thank you.'

'A different idea?' Butterflies swarmed her stomach, but she tried to quash them. Friendship only. That was to be the limit of her relationship with Duncan, she reminded herself. But there was nothing wrong with that, was there? After all, who didn't benefit from having another friend or two? 'What might that be exactly?'

'Well, to start with, you can put that computer away. We'll have these coffees and then you need to get your boots on. It's time you saw more of LochDarroch than the inside of this study.'

31

Duncan waited downstairs while Bex got ready. She wasn't entirely sure what she was supposed to wear, but boots probably meant jeans, too. As for picking out a top, she had brought a couple of items for wearing out – not that there was anywhere to go, but they were hardly suitable for exploring the Scottish countryside. And so, after a little deliberation, she chose a simple cream vest top with a chunky wooden necklace, although the moment she saw Duncan and the way his eyes widened, she feared she'd made the wrong choice.

'Is this not all right?' she asked, feeling a flutter of nerves.

'No, it's... You look... perfect,' he replied, a touch of awe in his voice.

'I think that might be a stretch,' she muttered, trying to ignore the warmth in her cheeks.

'It's not,' he insisted. 'Trust me.'

Silence swelled between them and Bex was sure she was meant to be the one to speak, only she didn't know how. She didn't want to think about how all her muscles seemed to have turned to jelly under his gaze, or how it would feel so straightforward just to take his hand and walk out of the castle, fingers interlocked. As she searched for something to say, she spotted the pair of amber eyes staring at her from behind Duncan.

'Are we okay to bring Ruby?' she said, stepping forwards, relieved to have a neutral conversation starter. 'She probably needs a walk, too.'

'Sure. But we have to swing by my lodge first,' he said. 'I need to grab a couple of things.'

As Bex followed Duncan out through one of the back doors of the castle, she was struck by just how little of the area she had explored. Not just outside, but inside the castle, too. Other than the first day when she had been looking for the study, she hadn't so much as peered in any other rooms, besides hers and the kitchen. And she knew there were other places worth exploring inside. What was it Duncan had called that room before? The solar? Maybe when she got a minute, she would see if she could find it. Although, if she had time to explore, then outside was probably the best place to do it.

'Wow, I thought the view from the front was incredible,' she said.

The door had opened onto the back lawns of the castle where a medley of greens stretched out as far as the eye could see, broken only by the crystal-blue water of the loch, while above the horizon, wisps of feathery cloud drifted lazily on the breeze.

'Yeah, you never get bored of it,' Duncan said. 'And every season is completely different. I love it in autumn, when all the trees start turning orange, and winter is stunning too, just freezing. Come on. I'm this way.'

They took a narrow stone path that weaved its way through dense pines. A shortcut, she realised, to the main road and the lodge house. Only when Duncan reached for his front door handle did Bex realise that leaving homes unlocked wasn't something only Fergus did.

'I'll just be a minute,' he said, opening the door only for his tone to change. 'Move out of the way, will you? Come on, you know I'm trying to get in.'

'So, this is the famous Kenna,' Bex said, keen to get a glimpse of Duncan's number one girl. Although when she did, she was forced to do a double take.

Down by his feet, blocking the door, was... well, it was a cat, but it was also the most enormous cat she had ever seen.

'Why is she so big?' she asked, unable to hide her shock. From nose to tail, the cat had to be a metre long, and that was a metre of pure muscle and fur. It was the type of cat she expected to see on a nature documentary, not standing in the doorway of Duncan's lodge. 'Is she some kind of special breed?'

'She's a Maine Coon,' Duncan replied. 'Which apparently means she requires constant attention and needs endless brushing.'

Bex watched as Duncan scooped the cat into his arms. So much for lifting logs to train. She was pretty sure that lifting a cat this size should be a weightlifting category.

'So, you really are a cat person,' she said.

'I think of myself as an animal person,' he said, gesturing towards Ruby, who had followed them into the house. 'She was supposed to be a Christmas gift for Lorna,' he explained, 'but it turns out Lorna doesn't like cats as much as she thought she did. And, as it happened, Kenna didn't like her much either. But she's all mine now, my very furry handful.' As he looked down at her, Kenna nuzzled her head into his beard. 'I'll give you a brush later, girl. I need to get something now.'

'I could give her a brush while you grab whatever you need.'

Bex heard the words leave her mouth before she could stop them.

'Are you sure?' Duncan asked. 'She'd love that. And it would stop her knocking everything off the shelf, the way she normally does when she doesn't get the fuss she's after. The brush is just over there.'

Bex looked over to where Duncan had gestured, wondering why the hell she had made the offer. Kenna looked like she could devour her whole. But there was no way she could back out now.

As Duncan dropped the giant feline onto the sofa, Bex picked up the brush, sat down beside the cat and tentatively began. Immediately, the purring started, encouraging Bex to brush just a little harder.

'Does her name mean something?' she asked as she focused on the long fur of the animal's tail. 'Kenna, it's pretty.'

'It's loosely from Gaelic,' Duncan replied. 'Meaning fire-born.'

'Because of her red fur?' Bex guessed.

'Sort of, but mainly because she was a fiery wee beast when she was a kitten. Could scratch like anything.'

'I find that hard to believe,' Bex replied as Kenna let out another low rumble.

'Oh, trust me, it's true.'

While Kenna's purring grew louder, Bex found herself surprisingly relaxed, entranced by the rhythmic brushing and the contentment of the oversized cat.

When she looked up, she saw Duncan still standing there, watching them with a soft smile.

'I thought you had to get something?' she said.

'Right, yes – getting on that now,' he said, snapping out of his reverie.

While Duncan disappeared, Bex remained on the sofa. Kenna had shifted her position so that her head was now resting on Bex's lap, while Ruby had laid herself flat across her feet. She was tempted to get a selfie, just to send to Claire and Daisy, but before she could work out how to get her phone without disturbing the animals, Duncan had returned, with a large, long bag slung over his shoulder.

Bex narrowed her eyes as she looked at the item.

'Should I know what that is?'

A slanted grin widened on Duncan's face.

'Don't worry, I'll show you,' he said. 'And I'm pretty sure you're going to love it.'

32

'What is that?'

Bex stared at the contraption in front of her, trying to work out what it was. They had walked away from the castle, down a thin path that weaved through the trees and bushes, until it opened onto an expanse of fields by the loch. From there, she had followed Duncan over several stiles and even through one kissing gate until he'd come to a stop a short way away from where the object stood and put down his bags, as if he'd expected her to understand what was going on. She'd never seen anything like it before. There was some sort of motor, by the looks of things, and six stacks of little round discs.

'It's a clay trap.'

'A what?'

Duncan's answer had left her absolutely none the wiser.

'For clay pigeon shooting,' he expanded. That, Bex had heard of.

During her years at the accountancy firm, Bex had been on hundreds of those damn workplace retreats where she was required to do archery and axe-throwing, normally after filling in endless questionnaires which resulted in being teamed up based on whatever colour, animal, or other personality profile was assigned. But she'd never done anything like this. She'd never even held a gun, let alone aimed one at something that was moving.

'I'm not sure I'll be any good at it,' she said hesitantly.

'Really? I get the impression you're the type of person who's good at everything.'

A light laugh escaped her. 'Okay, I am good at a lot of things, but that's normally because I use common sense and logic. I'm not sure that's going to work here.'

'You'd be surprised. Besides, I'm here to help you. Let's give it a go. As long as you're up for it. I mean, you can always go back to the study and keep working on those accounts if you want?'

His smirk was infuriating, not to mention attractive. Of course she didn't want to go back into the study. It was stunning out here and the crisp clean air was a far cry from the stagnant, dust-filled atmosphere she had been working in all week.

'Okay,' she said after a pause. 'But if I'm not any good, then I'll blame you for being a terrible teacher.'

'Of course you will,' he replied. 'Now, protection first.'

'Protection?'

From out of his bag, he pulled two pairs of fawn-coloured defenders.

'May I?'

Bex nodded, assuming Duncan was going to hand her the ear defenders, but instead, he moved closer towards her, raised his hands and gently brushed a strand of hair behind her ears.

'Hopefully these fit okay,' he said, the gravelly tone in his voice resonating all the way through her. Once again, she nodded, having apparently lost the ability to speak. 'So before we fire the clays, we need to work on your position and mounting the gun. Now, be careful not to pull the trigger. I've just loaded.'

A flurry of nerves cascaded through her. She'd never considered herself clumsy before. But then, she'd never been given a loaded shotgun to hold before, either.

'So, place your left hand here,' Duncan said. His voice was a gentle, warm whisper in her ear as he rested his palm on the back of her hand. Bex tried to ignore the tingle that was spreading on that side of her face and focus on listening to what he was saying. But it wasn't easy. She just seemed to dissolve into his lilting accent. 'Great, and now you're going to lift it up, so that your cheek bone is lying flat against it there, that's it. You don't need to tilt your head. You've got it.'

Bex wasn't aware she had tilted her head. Actually, she wasn't aware of any movements her body was doing at all, and she sure as hell wasn't in control of them. It was taking all her willpower not to be distracted by the constant shivers running down her spine as Duncan's chest pressed up against her back.

'Sorry, but I need to get this close to do it properly,' he said, as if he was reading her mind.

'Really?'

'Well, it's definitely the easiest way of doing it, but I'd be lying if I said I hadn't picked something that meant I'd get to be close to you. Just tell me if you want to move.'

He was giving her a way out, but more than that, he was reading her. Seeing if she wanted him close to her the same way he did.

'If this is the best way to learn, then I'll just have to cope,' she said, trying to stop the smile from flickering on her lips.

'Don't worry, I'll only hold you like this until you've got the hang of it. You need to be able to feel the recoil and allow your body to move without losing control.'

'Right,' Bex said, wishing her voice didn't sound quite so breathy. 'Of course.'

'Now, just squeeze there. That's all you're doing, squeezing gently.'

'There's nothing to shoot at,' she said, forcing herself to swallow. It may have been summer, but even so the heat was stifling.

'Don't worry, we'll get the hang of this first, then I'll do the clays,' Duncan said, still holding her close. 'Just squeeze a little more.'

Finally, Bex did as instructed and pulled the trigger.

The force with which the gun recoiled was far stronger than she'd expected, and she found herself pushed back into Duncan's chest. A rush of adrenaline bolted through her, though she didn't know if it was from firing a gun or the fact that his body was so close.

'How did that feel?' Duncan asked.

'How did...?' She took a second to realise he was talking about the gun, and not his arms around her. 'Good,' she said, her pulse still pounding against her ears. 'I mean, yes, yes, that was... yes, good.'

'Okay, right, well, I'm going to try letting a clay go now.'

In her flustered state, she had stepped away from Duncan, yet it was only as he moved across to the trap that she felt that distance between them.

'The key is to make sure you keep the gun mounted like I showed you,' he said. 'The clay's going to go up in the air, and you're going to follow it with your eyes and your gun. Keep moving them together, and when you feel ready, squeeze that trigger again. Ready?'

'Probably not,' she replied truthfully.

'I'll take that as a yes.'

The first shot was a bust. As the small disk rose through the air, Bex continued following it, keeping the gun in the position Duncan had shown her, waiting for the moment she felt comfortable enough to pull the trigger. Only just when she thought she was ready, the clay slowed and began its descent, and suddenly she was all off balance. In a rash attempt to save herself from failure, she swung the shotgun down, losing sight of the clay as she finally pulled the trigger.

'I think it's safe to say I'm not a natural at this,' she said.

'That was your first attempt,' he said. 'You just need to go for it sooner. Let's reload and go again.'

Bex followed every instruction Duncan gave her to a tee, and after twenty minutes of hit and misses, she struck three clays in a row. After that, they paused to eat the sandwiches he had brought with him, then they started again.

Straight off the bat, Bex hit four shots, but then it started going downhill.

'I think this is where we have to end it,' she said, having missed her third consecutive clay. 'I think I've peaked.'

'You're just tired. I think you're a natural.' Duncan grinned, taking the gun from her and holding out his hand for the ear defenders, too.

'No, you don't.' Bex laughed back.

'No, okay, maybe not a natural, but I think with a bit of work you wouldn't be bad at this.'

Bex looked out into the sky, at the miles and miles of blue. 'So, do you shoot other things too?' she said. 'I mean, like pheasants or deer?'

'No, that's not my thing,' Duncan said, crinkling his nose. 'Strange, I know, for a country boy, but I'm perfectly happy with the clays.'

A warmth rose through Bex at the thought of this burly man

with his giant cat and aversion to shooting living things. He was full of surprises, that was for sure.

'So, given that I helped you this morning, that means I've almost worked off my five days, right?'

'You didn't help,' Bex said. 'You brought me gifts and stopped me from doing work. Technically, because of you, I'm behind where I would have been. Anyway, the five days just restarted.'

'What?' Duncan's jaw dropped, eyes widening. 'Why?'

'Well, because of this,' she said, gesturing to where they were standing.

'This?'

'This. This was absolutely a date,' she said. 'We went somewhere, just the two of us, we did something fun together, and you brought me food. That's a date.'

'Oh, Barker, this was not a date,' he said. 'Trust me. When you and I are on a date, you will know.'

'Is that right?'

The butterflies were swarming in her stomach again, trying to push her towards him. She was an arm's length away at most. A few small steps and she could be pressed up against his chest.

'Well, I'm booking a table for Friday,' Duncan said, breaking her stream of thoughts before she could do anything stupid. 'I'm taking you for dinner.'

Dinner with Duncan. Was that what she wanted? She knew his situation, and Lorna had specifically warned her off, but really, how well did she know Lorna? It wasn't like they were close friends; they had just met.

Bex stepped back, shaking her head as she moved. No, that wasn't the type of person Lorna was. Besides, she had already arranged to meet her again. Next Friday.

'No can do, I'm afraid,' she said, leaning in. 'I'm going out with your sister then. Lorna said it's the only evening she's free.'

'Oh, is that right?'

'Yes.' Relief billowed through Bex at having a justifiable reason to say no to Duncan's request, without having to find any willpower of her own. Yet as the smirk rose on his lips, she suspected she might not have got out of the situation quite as easily as she'd hoped.

'I guess I'll just have to check with her if I can come then, won't I?' he said. 'And just so you know, Lorna never says no to her big brother.' With that, he slipped the gun back into its bag, flashed her another smile, then began walking back up towards the lodge.

33

Duncan offered to walk Bex and Ruby back up to the castle, but given that he would just have to go back on himself afterwards, it seemed unnecessary. Still, as they reached the lodge door, he stopped and lingered outside.

'I'm sure Kenna would like it if you came in and said hello to her again,' he said. 'With all that fuss you gave her, I'm not going to stop hearing the end of it until she sees you again.'

Bex had to make a concerted effort not to look at that smile twisting up the corners of his lips. It seemed to have the ability to melt all her resolve.

'Is that right?' Bex laughed. The fact that a man was using his cat as an excuse to see her again was ridiculous – but she couldn't help but find it very sweet.

'Well, I'm here for a very long time,' she reminded him. 'I'm sure I'll get to see her again at some point.'

'And what about me? I guess now you've got your coffee machine and papers sorted, you've no need for me any more.'

Bex froze and tipped her head to the side, offering him a look of deep confusion.

'Have you forgotten about my lunch?' she said. 'I was getting used to those sandwiches and bridies. Don't tell me I'm going to have to make my own food now?'

Duncan threw back his head and laughed. He had one of those laughs that could lift the entire mood of a room. She had always been envious of people like that. People who could effortlessly put others at ease. Her friend Claire had the same skill. She was full of warm words and genuine empathy. As she looked at Duncan, all she could feel was the smile taking a deeper and deeper hold of her.

'I really am sorry about the other night,' Duncan said, his expression far more serious. 'At the pub, with Katty. You didn't see my best side at all.'

'No,' she agreed.

'But hopefully you're seeing that's not what I'm like. Not normally.'

It was true. Of all the times she had spoken to Duncan, it was only that once he had shown himself as a red flag. But people could mask what they were feeling, and it would be easy for him to believe he was over Katty, because he was focusing his attention on Bex. But if he was needing to focus his attention on someone else to believe he was over his ex, then he really wasn't over her at all.

'I've had a good day, Duncan,' she said. 'Thank you.'

She turned around and began walking up the gravel path towards the house. 'See you soon?' Duncan's voice called from behind her.

'Maybe.' She laughed, waving her hand without so much as a backwards glance.

As she strolled the last part of the path up to the house, she couldn't help but feel a slight lightness to her step. And while at no point in her life had Bex ever envisioned herself as a whistling person, there was something about her mood – or maybe it was the scenery, or just the fresh air – that made a tune buzz through her head. Yes, regardless of Duncan or the state of the job, she was going to make sure she took time out of every day to head outside. Just for half an hour or so. It would be good for her mental health. And if she happened to bump into the groundskeeper on those strolls, then so be it.

She pushed open the front door of the castle, ready to head upstairs and perhaps soak in the tub, when her name was called from inside the drawing room.

'Rebecca.'

Fergus's gruff tone seemed to lean all the attention on the last two syllables of her name, missing the first one entirely. 'You got a wee minute?'

Bex's good mood evaporated and was replaced by an uneasy chill. Remaining where she was, she glanced down at Ruby, contemplating what she should do. Technically speaking, it was Saturday, and there was no reason at all that she should be expected to work. Any requests Fergus had could wait until Monday morning, and she was tempted to say as much – but this was his home, and she was going to be here for a long time. Given how they'd already got off to a fairly rocky start, she decided it was probably best to at least see what he wanted, even if she wasn't going to do anything about it until after the weekend.

With a deep breath in, she pushed open the door to the drawing room.

'Hi, Fergus, is there anything I can help you with?'

She was using her professional voice – the one she reserved for entitled clients who always thought they knew best, though if they did, there would have been no need to hire her in the first place.

Fergus was sitting in the same armchair, and even though it was only ten past four, he had a large tumbler of whisky at his side.

As he looked at her, his eyes narrowed.

'Aye,' he said. 'I wondered if you an' I could have a word.'

He picked up the empty glass beside him and tipped it towards the chair in front of him.

'Sit,' he said.

34

Bex didn't have to sit. She knew that. She reminded herself of what she'd thought only a moment before. This was her weekend, and she didn't have to do anything she didn't want to. But there was something about the way Fergus had spoken that had her intrigued. His face was off in a daze, and she couldn't help but wonder when he had last had someone to sit and talk to in here.

She hesitated for a moment longer, then finally, taking her time, strode slowly across the room and sat down.

Silence swirled around them. From her seat on the floor, Ruby's gaze moved between Fergus and Bex and back again as if she wasn't sure what was going on. *You're not the only one*, Bex thought, although rather than saying as much, she cleared her throat and forced that professional smile back onto her lips.

'Is everything all right?' she asked. 'If you've been in the study, you'll have seen I've made a lot of progress in there. The personal things are all set aside, though. I can show you where they are if you need them.'

He grunted in a way that could have been a yes or a no. Bex

clamped her mouth shut. She wasn't going to say any more. He was the one who had asked to speak to her. So he could bloody well speak.

Out in the hallway, the grandfather clock struck to announce a quarter past the hour. She had been in here for nearly five minutes and he had said absolutely nothing. Finally, the old man coughed.

'So, you went out with the boy today,' he said.

'You mean Duncan? Yes, he was just showing me how to clay pigeon shoot.'

'Is that right?'

She didn't know how to respond to that comment either. Of course that was right. That was why she had said it. She was just about to ask if there was a particular reason he had called her in here, other than to make her feel as awkward as possible, when he spoke again.

'He's a hard worker, that one.'

'I can imagine. I heard you used to be friends with his grand-father,' she said, only to regret the comment. Why on earth would she have brought that up when she knew they had stopped speaking? 'Sorry, I shouldn't be nosy.'

'Not nosy,' he said. ''t's taking an interest. It's what people do.' He paused, filling up the glass he'd held out to Bex earlier, then passed it across to her. She wasn't much of a whisky drinker, but she needed something to take the edge of this conversation. 'Aye we used to be friends. Different time back then. Different place too. This—' The way he nodded, it felt like he was talking about the whole castle. Or maybe, Bex thought, thinking of the photo with him laughing away, he was referring to himself. Maybe he had felt like a different person back then, too.

She took a sip of her drink. The smoky caramel taste was followed by a heat down the back of her throat, which wasn't anywhere near as unpleasant as she'd imagined. As such, she took another, slightly longer sip immediately after. When she looked up, Fergus had the faintest whisper of a smile gracing his lips.

'Shall I top that up a dram for ye?' he said, eyeing the glass in her hand. Bex was surprised by how much she had drunk. Or how nice it was. She hesitated. All she had eaten all day was the sandwich that Duncan had brought them, and she'd been planning on making some eggs for dinner, but there were a couple of hours until then. She could sit and have another drink with Fergus. Especially if it improved the relationship between them.

'Just a little,' she said, and held out her glass. When her gaze met Fergus's, she saw a twinkle in his eye. A twinkle she had never seen before.

'Aye, just a wee dram,' he replied, then proceeded to pour the drink.

* * *

She should have stopped at least two drinks ago. Probably three. But she was having fun. Genuinely. And as the latest laugh barrelled from Fergus, it was so loud and unexpected that one of the dogs started howling.

'Why do I get the feeling they're not used to hearing you make this noise?' Bex asked.

'Daft buggers, they are,' Fergus said, ruffling the dog behind the ears with a rough stroke.

They had been speaking for two hours, although when the conversation had shifted from polite small talk – how long the castle had been in Fergus's family, how big the village was, how long she had been at her firm, etc. – to this – amusing anecdotes from their lives – Bex couldn't be sure. And by amusing anecdotes from their lives, she meant Fergus's. The old man certainly had tales to tell.

'Well, after that, my days as the caber toss champion were gone. Still had to go along to the events though. I may have tried to spread a rumour that he cheated, but no one was buying that.' His gruff chuckle continued, pausing only as he took another draw from his drink.

The latest tales he'd been telling Bex were those where he had joined in the highland games, and judging by what she'd heard so far, the caber toss and shot putt were mere sidelines to all the things they got up to.

'And where was Winny when you were up to all this?' Bex asked, keen to hear more about the wife that she had heard of only as a 'marriage of convenience'.

'Oh, she was there,' he said. 'Normally with the bairns. Treated all the wee ones in the village like they were family. Think it happens like that a lot when you can't have your own.'

The laughter faded, and for the first time a quiet sadness permeated the air. There was so much more Bex wanted to ask Fergus. She wanted to ask how he had come to be living on his own in such a great castle; she wanted to know what had happened with Duncan's grandfather and why Fergus had stayed so close to Duncan, though she suspected she already knew the answer to that. Guilt. He might not have been able to put things right with his best friend, but he could try to build the bridges with his grandson. Make amends for a fractured past in the only way he could. With the drink loosening her tongue, she was more than a little tempted to dig into that particular strand of his past. But instead, she asked a different question, though it was still related to family.

'I've heard a couple of people mention your nephew, Kieron,' she said. 'Is he on your side of the family, or Winny's?'

'Ah, now Kieron is my sister Ishbel's boy.' A smile broadened on his face. 'She's a special lass, my Ishbel. Firecracker that's for sure. Unlike that lad of hers. Takes after his dad, that one.' He let out a low hiss, and Bex found herself reminded of when she had mentioned Kieron to Duncan. There was clearly some friction there.

'Right, enough o' this, I'm going to give you some words o' wisdom,' Fergus said, lifting his glass. 'Call it payment for drinkin' all my best whisky.'

'Shouldn't I be the one paying you, if it's for the whisky?' Bex asked, aware of the fact that the floor seemed to have developed ever such a slight sway. Yet Fergus merely waved his hand at her as he shook his head.

'Dinnae wait,' he said. 'Whatever you're thinking about doing, dinnae wait. Do it now. You don't ken if you're going to get a tomorrow, or if it's going to be the tomorrow you think you ought to have. So dinnae wait. That's it. That's my advice.' He brought his glass to his lips as if he was going to take a sip, only to change his mind and continue talking. 'Oh, aye, and make the big memories.'

'Big memories?'

'Aye, it's no' the big things, it's the big memories. The ones that stop your heart. That you remember even when you're my age and the drink's weathered half yer heid. Like that darn caber toss.' He let out a chuckle. 'And the way she, she...' He shuddered his shoulders, drawing the rest of his sentence back within him, before he looked back to Bex. 'Like I said, it's the big memories that stick. An' if you're no' careful, they might pass y' by before y' even notice.'

There was something about the way his eyes drifted off into nothing that made Bex think Fergus was no longer thinking about the caber toss. There was a wistfulness to his gaze as he stared into the last dregs of his drink. Was it Winny perhaps? Or maybe someone who had come before his wife? The woman in the photograph with Duncan's grandfather, maybe.

Before she could ask, Ruby let out a long yawn and looked up at Bex with her big amber eyes. Aware of the gaze still on her, Bex glanced down at her watch. Somehow it was gone seven. She had spent three hours talking to Fergus and still hadn't eaten anything. Suddenly aware of how empty her stomach was feeling, she slowly stood up, resting her hand on the arm of the sofa to help with the sudden unevenness of the floor.

'I should leave you in peace,' Bex said. 'Although I was going to make an omelette for dinner. I bought some eggs yesterday, if you fancy one too?'

Fergus smiled at her warmly.

'You're all right, lass,' he said. 'I'll have a wander up to the village in a bit. Let these guys stretch their legs.'

'I'll see you tomorrow then. Goodnight, Fergus.'

'Goodnight, lass.'

It turned out that making an omelette after numerous whiskies was easier said than done. The first attempt had to be binned, due to the half a shell that ended up in the mixture. Even on the second attempt, what Bex ended up with was far closer to scrambled egg. Dry scrambled egg with no sauce and nothing to make it taste better. On Monday, when the shops were open again, she was going to need to do a proper shop, even if it meant taking an hour lunch break to get it done.

As she climbed up the stairs towards her bed half an hour later, her conversation with Fergus was still playing on her mind. What were her big memories? There was the memory of her parents' thirtieth wedding anniversary that had happened the year before. That felt like a big one, as did the memory of Theo proposing to Daisy, not to mention their wedding, but they didn't feel like they should be her memories. They were theirs. Immediately, an image flickered into her mind: Duncan opening the bathroom door while she was standing in there naked. That one seemed unlikely to fade soon. If ever. What about him bringing the bridie? Or the way he had held her body close to his while he had shown her how to mount the gun, then added the gentle pressure to her finger as he guided her to squeeze the trigger? No, she thought, trying to push the images from her mind. He was a friend. A friend who brought her food and gifts and made her feel like her entire body was on fire every time they touched. People had friends like that, didn't they?

She dropped onto the bed, only for Ruby to let out a low whine that perfectly encapsulated how Bex felt. There was no point denying it. She didn't see Duncan as a friend. She never had. But he was also definitely not boyfriend material either. Not given his current state, so where did that leave her?

'I know, girl,' Bex said, reaching down to scratch beneath the dog's chin. 'I seem to have found myself in a bit of a pickle here.'

35

Bex's head hurt. Really hurt. Apparently, the burned scrambled egg had done nothing to absorb all the alcohol from the whisky. Thankfully, even in her state, she remembered the earplugs Duncan had gifted her, and as such, it was nearly midday by the time she woke up. So late that even Ruby had gone.

Even with the pounding behind her temples and the foul furry taste in her mouth, she could feel the effects of a decent night's sleep for the first time since she had moved here.

With a stretch and a yawn, Bex rolled over and picked up her phone, only to see that Lorna had set up a group chat entitled 'Lion Friday Night'.

7pm. Can't wait to see you.

Blunt and to the point. It was the type of message Bex liked, although she couldn't help but notice that Duncan's name was on the list, too. Not only that, but he'd sent her a message too.

> She said I could crash. Hope you don't mind.
> And I'm not counting this as a date.

She laughed. Even in her mind, she had to agree this wasn't a date. Just a drink at the pub. Besides, it was a week away. By that time, she might have completely forgotten about this crush. After all, she had gone off guys far quicker than that in the past. It was perfectly possible, wasn't it?

* * *

No. Bex discovered when Friday rolled around, it was not possible to be over a crush on someone like Duncan. Not that quickly, anyway.

Unlike the week before, they hadn't spent much time together, but whenever she did see him, it set her pulse racing. Like the morning she looked out of her window and saw him there, chasing the dogs around, rubbing their tummies and letting them jump all over him. There was something so endearing about the moment. Clearly, he thought no one was looking, and she couldn't help but smile at the sight of him behaving like a big kid.

Then there was the bridie he'd left by her coffee machine on Tuesday. She had been so absorbed working, she'd had no idea when he'd come into the castle, or if he'd even come to the study to speak to her, but when she went to make herself a drink a little after one, there was a brown paper bag and a small note beside it.

So you remember to eat.

That didn't help her crush, either.

Then there was the way he was with Fergus. One evening, midweek, she had just curled up into bed when she heard the laughter rolling from downstairs, and a whole new sense of warmth took a hold of her. A warmth that increased the next morning when she went down, found the door to the drawing room open, and Fergus there in his chair, with a blanket laid carefully across him, a pillow beneath his head and a glass of water where his whisky would normally be. Bex suspected this wasn't the first time Duncan had done this for the old man, and the knowledge only made those damn butterflies increase.

By the time Friday had come around, she found herself over-thinking what she was going to wear, which was a far cry from when she'd first gone for a drink with Lorna when she'd barely had time for a shower.

Knowing that Duncan had complimented her in jeans, she chose a similar outfit, but paired it with heels. And after popping her head in the drawing room to say goodbye to Fergus and take Ruby down to him so that she wasn't up all night waiting for her, she left for the village.

Bex arrived at the Lion five minutes early, exactly as she had planned. Being early let her get a sense of the room, maybe even work out escape routes if she needed.

This time, though, she was using those extra minutes to decide where to sit. Did she want to sit next to Duncan? No. This was not a date. Absolutely not a date. Besides, she didn't know how much Lorna knew about her having spent time with Duncan, and she wanted to get to know Lorna, Eilidh and Niall better. Yes, the aim was to sit one place away from Duncan. That would make it harder for them to talk directly, and she wouldn't be facing him. That was if the table was round, of course – if it was rectangular, she'd need another plan. Knowing that Lorna had booked them a table, she was about to ask the barman which was theirs, only for Eilidh and Niall to arrive at the same time.

'It feels like it's been forever,' Eilidh said, wrapping Bex in a hug the moment she saw her. 'How's it going? How's life at the castle?'

'Much of the same – lots of paperwork, but I think I'm through the worst of it, which is good.'

'You're done?' Niall said. 'You mean...?'

'Oh God, no.' Bex laughed. 'I mean, I've just sorted out which of the thousand pieces of paper are rubbish and which I need to use in the accounts. I've still got weeks left to go.'

'Well, that's good for us at least,' Eilidh said, 'to have more time to see you. And Lorna will be glad too – she's gutted that she had to miss tonight.'

'Lorna's not coming?' The surprise lifted in Bex's voice.

'Didn't you see her message? Her car broke down just outside Glasgow on her way back from work. I offered to go and get her, but she said she'd be fine. So it's just gonna be the four of us – is that a problem?'

'No, no problem,' Bex said. 'I mean, I'm guessing Duncan's still coming?'

'Judging by the way he's walking towards us right now, I'd say yes.'

Bex turned around, and yes, Duncan was walking straight over. For a moment, all she could do was stand there and take him in. He was dressed in a pale blue shirt that complemented his colouring while his hair was half up, in a style that she would have thought of as feminine, but on him emanated 100 per cent raw masculine energy. How had she never noticed exactly how utterly piercing his eyes were? Or how broad his shoulders were, either? He was, without a shadow of a doubt, absolutely freaking gorgeous. As her eyes inadvertently locked on his, he flashed her a smile that caused all the muscles in her abdomen to clench.

'The four of us?' Bex said, swallowing back the racing in her chest. 'No, no, that sounds absolutely great.'

36

Bex was too stunned by Duncan's appearance to think straight as Eilidh and Niall instinctively slipped in next to each other at the table, meaning she was next to Duncan. Maybe it was better this way – better than having to look straight at him the entire time. How was he so damn attractive? His cheekbones were as sharp as the axes she had imagined him chopping with, and those damn eyes – the candlelight from the table was obviously doing something to them, Making them even more mesmerising. Not that she kept looking at them. Or at least, she hoped she didn't.

This pub had a very different atmosphere from the White Hart. This, in her opinion, anyway, was more of a gastropub, where people were coming for the food and the atmosphere, rather than just a place to catch up with their friends and a pint.

'The haggis here is great,' Eilidh said as they browsed the menus. 'I'm not sure if you've had haggis yet, but if you're going to try it, I'd definitely recommend it here.'

'Well, I really like bridies,' Bex replied. 'Duncan's brought me them for lunch a couple of times.'

Bex only realised what she'd said a moment after the words

slipped out. Fingers crossed it wouldn't get back to Lorna that Duncan had brought her lunch, although from Eilidh's response, she didn't seem to notice anything odd about the comment.

'Really? Oh wow, we're already turning you into a local!' Eilidh laughed.

'Well, I wouldn't go that far, but yeah, trying haggis sounds like a good idea.'

'Don't worry about driving,' Niall said. 'I've got work early tomorrow, so I can drop you home.'

'I brought my car,' Bex replied. She had ummed and ahhed about walking, but the heels had cinched it for her. Dry weather or not, she was likely to twist an ankle on all the gravel and cobblestones. Besides, the last thing she needed was to have too much to drink in front of Duncan while there were other people there.

'Well, if you decide you want a couple, your car'll be fine to leave overnight,' Niall assured her.

'I'll remember that,' Bex said, although at that moment, her mind was a million miles away from the thought of getting home, or even whether she wanted to enjoy a couple of drinks.

Instead, all she could focus on was the fact that Duncan was seated just inches from her, and every time she moved slightly, their thighs brushed. Sometimes it was just for a brief moment, but at other times, like now, the moment lingered, causing her breath to stutter.

She needed to stop thinking about it. She needed to stop thinking about how easy it would be to slip her hand onto his knee or intertwine her fingers with his. This was ridiculous.

'So, what is it you do?' she asked Niall, desperate to distract herself from the feel of Duncan's eyes constantly looking at her.

'Oh, it's not very interesting at all. I work in farm machinery.'

'What do you mean, "not interesting"?' Eilidh said. 'He's downplaying how hard he works massively. He's already a director at the company.'

'Wow, that's great going,' Bex said.

Niall shrugged. 'I know, but Eilidh makes it sound better than it is – I mean, it's a company of three people. Two of us are directors.'

'It's still a company,' Bex said. 'Most people don't have the courage to take risks like that.'

'Is it something you'd do?' Duncan asked. 'Start your own business?'

Bex considered the question. 'The thing with accountancy firms in London is that there are so many big names, going on your own is just career suicide unless you've got a massive client list that'll come with you, and even then there are all these non-compete agreements.'

'You don't have to do it in London,' Duncan said. 'Surely you could set up somewhere else, somewhere that needs an accountancy firm.'

'Like here?' Eilidh suggested, voicing the unspoken idea that Duncan had implied. 'That would be amazing! Set up an accountancy firm here.'

'I'm not sure there'd be enough business for me around here once I'm done with Fergus's castle books.' Bex laughed, unsure if she liked the way all the attention had currently shifted to her. But then, what had she expected? They already knew everything about each other. To them, she was the interesting one.

'Are you kidding?' Niall said. 'Loads of businesses around here need help. We'd employ you and I'd bet my right leg I'm not the only one. I'd bet there's an absolute goldmine here for someone with your skills.'

'And she's amazing, honestly. An absolute work horse.'

The compliment came from Duncan, and when Bex turned to look at him, she couldn't help but feel a smile lift in her eyes. Not to mention a flurry of butterflies in her abdomen. Still, it was Niall's comment that played on her mind.

Bex thought about it. When she had first started out, being the director of her own accountancy firm had been the long-term goal, but then, since she'd learned more about the business, she'd shifted her mindset to assuming she'd stay at Smiths and Bears. After all, the fact that she was here was a sign of how many hoops she was willing to jump through for them.

'I'm happy where I am for now,' she said.

'Oh well, we've still got a few weeks to persuade you otherwise, right?'

'Yes, we do,' Duncan replied, flashing her another of those grins.

Eilidh laughed before picking up the wine bottle and topping up Bex's glass, followed by her own. Perhaps Bex would grab that lift from Niall after all.

The rest of the meal passed with constant chatter and laughter, with the only quiet moments coming when they were all digging into their food. Just as the others had said, the haggis was delicious, as were all the side dishes, which only helped the wine flow even faster. As did the fact that she needed something in her hand to stop it from accidentally brushing up against Duncan.

The first time it happened was when they both went for the water jug at the same time, then again when she reached across him to get the salt. She had finished her main course when she reached out to get her glass only to find she had picked up his instead. A fact he let her know by gently stroking the top of her knuckles. And when she dropped her napkin, he was the one who reached down and picked it up, only for his arm to graze the outside of her thigh, which caused her pulse to rocket as a flash of heat flooded her entire body. It was a far cry from the way he had been slinging his arm across her the last time they had been in the pub together. The gestures were so small, so intimate, they were probably imperceptible to anyone else, and at times, Bex had to remind herself that there were other people around the table too. Not just her and Duncan. Something she managed by keeping the conversation going as much as possible.

'One of my best friends is a painter,' Bex said when she learned Eilidh was a textile artist. 'She does it part-time and runs a café, but she's absolutely incredible. I have to show you some of her paintings. Hold on a sec.'

She flicked through her phone to find photos of Daisy's watercolours, then passed it over to Niall and Eilidh to look at. As she did, she felt Duncan's gaze lingering on her.

'Your friends mean the world to you, don't they?' he said.

'Yes, they do. We've been best friends since we were kids. I don't think anything can ever replace relationships like that.' As soon as the words left her mouth, she knew what she'd said. What was it with her putting her foot in it? No doubt Duncan's Friday nights used to be spent with his best friends too, before everything had happened. And once again, she had reminded him of that.

'I'm sorry, I didn't mean—'

'No, it's fine, really.' He smiled, his eyes fixed on hers. 'You're right; it is lucky to have friendships like that. But that doesn't mean you shouldn't open yourself up to what else is out there. Don't you think?'

'Maybe.'

Their eyes were locked on one another again. As if the rest of the room was just a vignette, blurring out of focus, so all that mattered was them.

'Those are incredible,' Eilidh said, handing Bex her phone back and breaking the moment. 'She's so talented.'

Bex cleared her throat. 'Right, I know. She's phenomenal.' She cast another quick glance at Duncan, unsure why it was so hard to look away from him. But considering the number of times their eyes had met, she was pretty sure she wasn't the only one having the issue.

Still, for the first time all night, silence threatened to take hold of the table, but before it could, Niall lifted his hand to his mouth to cover a wide yawn.

'Guys, I hate to do this, but I think I've got to head off. It was an early one this morning.'

'I was thinking the same,' Eilidh said. 'And you're giving me a lift back, so I guess that's my sign that I'm going too. What about you two? Do you want a lift?'

Bex knew what she wanted. She wanted Duncan to say they would finish off their wine. Subtext for spending time alone together. But it was reckless of her to want that, wasn't it?

Still, she glanced at him, hoping to read his expression to see if he wanted the same. Yet before he spoke, Eilidh's phone pinged.

'It's Lorna,' she said, glancing down at the screen. 'She's just checking we're all having a good night and not having too much fun without her.'

A pang of guilt shot through Bex. Lorna had been so good to her, including her in their friendship circle, checking on her at the castle. And she'd asked only one thing – that Bex steer clear of Duncan. Bex tried to ignore the tension buzzing between them as she turned to him.

'You know what, I think I'm going to head back too,' she said. 'I thought I might go for a walk by the loch tomorrow.'

'Really? Do you want some company?' Duncan asked.

She smiled but shook her head, surprised at how blatant he had been in front of the others. There was no chance that wouldn't get back to Lorna.

'Thank you, but I'm not sure what time I'll be going. If it's raining, I'll go later, and I don't want to mess you around.' She could feel the tension simmering between them. 'It's fine, really. But I should get home now.'

'Right, of course.'

'So do you guys want a lift?' Niall offered.

Bex readied herself to accept the offer, but before she spoke, Duncan cut in.

'Actually, I was going to walk,' he said. 'As it's a nice evening. Bex, do you want to join me?'

She did – she desperately did – but it was the wrong thing to do. She knew it was the wrong thing to do.

But she had already declined his offer to join her at the loch tomorrow and they had all heard. Walking home with him now was harmless, surely? Particularly since they practically lived in the same place. A bubble of apprehension threatened to rise and make her see sense, but before she could contemplate all the reasons that Duncan walking her home was a bad idea, she quashed it.

'Why not?' she said, flashing him a smile. 'Although just so you know, I'm in heels, so it's going to be a very slow walk back.'

'Oh, I'm sure I'll cope,' he said, grinning back at her.

37

Given how easily they normally spoke, the silence between them as they walked back to the castle felt notably tense. In Bex's case, it had everything to do with their hands. Several times, she almost reached out to hold Duncan's only to snap her hand back to her side. She was sure he did the same. So they opted to walk a couple of feet apart, which was ridiculous, really.

'That was a nice night, wasn't it?' Bex said, aware of how oddly formal she sounded.

'Aye, they're grand, those two. Good mates, too.'

'Lorna thinks there's something going on between them. Or at least there should be. And I'm inclined to agree, don't you think?'

'Maybe there could be,' Duncan said, 'but maybe they're wiser than that. I mean, if they're just friends, maybe they don't want to ruin it.'

'But would it be ruining the friendship? It could be something so much more—'

'Or it could end up an absolute disaster.'

She saw a flicker of pain cross his face, and the guilt rolled through her. So many times now she had ended up putting her foot in her mouth, or feeling like she was about to, but maybe what she actually needed to do was talk to Duncan about what he'd been through. And not the fact that he had been cheated on, but how he had lost the people closest to him.

'Do you not talk to Archie at all?' she asked before she could stop herself. 'He was your best friend. Surely you miss him, too?'

It was intrusive, possibly rude, but she wanted to know. Duncan was such a people person, the type everyone gravitated towards. It was hard to imagine him cutting someone out of his life entirely.

'He's tried calling a couple of times,' Duncan admitted, his gaze drifting down to his feet. 'But what would I say to him? I need to move on with my life, and he needs to move on with his. I suppose I should be the bigger person and forgive him or something, but—'

'No, I think you're being the bigger person as it is,' Bex said. 'The fact that you haven't wrung his neck or beaten him to a pulp shows real restraint,' she added, then paused. 'You didn't, did you?'

Duncan laughed. 'No, I didn't. That's not to say I didn't think about it, but I decided that wouldn't be a good idea.'

'What about Katty? Have you spoken to her?'

He shook his head. 'She still messages, but it's the same – I don't have anything to say to her. The truth is, I think it was inevitable, her and me drifting apart. If I'm honest with myself, I think part of me knew that, even when I proposed. Maybe that was *why* I proposed.'

'What?' Bex stopped. Partly because her feet were killing her, but also because she didn't think this was the type of thing you shared just strolling along. She wanted to look at Duncan as he told her this. To show him she was listening. With a slight nod of his head, he paused and looked around at her.

'Katty has always been too big for a village like this – same as Archie has. You saw her, right? She never really fit in.'

'I could see that,' Bex admitted. 'But I'm hardly one to comment. It's not like I fit in here either.'

'From where I'm looking, you're doing a pretty good job.' He smiled, but it was with his lips alone. His eyes were shadowed. 'But Katty... I think I could feel she was outgrowing this place, and I wanted to keep her here. So I proposed.'

'She didn't have to say yes, though,' Bex countered. 'If she thought she was outgrowing the place, surely it would've been kinder to turn you down.'

'Maybe,' he replied. 'But maybe she didn't want to outgrow it. Maybe she was trying to use me as her anchor to stay. I don't know. It's strange, though... These last few months, of course I've been lonely, but it's more that I miss having someone to talk to. Someone to wake up with in the morning. I don't think I've actually missed *her*.'

'Wow,' Bex said. 'Those are strong words.'

'I know. Maybe the wine's to blame.' He chuckled, then met her gaze to prove that wasn't the point at all.

'So, is that why you hang out with me?' Bex said. 'To fill that gap?' She couldn't hide the pang of disappointment that struck behind her ribcage. But what did she expect? She had known he was in serious rebound territory from that first day.

'Yes... but no,' he said. 'It's not just that. I do like having you to talk to, but with you, it's different. You make me laugh, and when you're not there, it's not like anyone else can just step in and replace you. It's you I want to be with.'

'Duncan...'

'I know, I know – you don't want to hear this and I get that.

But I want to be honest with you. There's something so special about you. And I don't just mean the fact that you have a fricking beautiful body.'

'Hey, I thought you said you didn't see anything,' she said, laughing as she slapped him playfully on the arm, only for him to hold her by the wrist.

That was when the laughter stopped, and it was just them, staring into one another's eyes. Could he really be looking at her like that if all she was to him was a rebound? And what did that say about all the other men she had dated? Because she was pretty sure that none of them had ever looked at her like that before.

'I like spending time with you too,' she said softly.

As they stood there, he lifted his hand and brushed a strand of hair behind her ears. Her eyes closed involuntarily as she drew in a long breath. Pine. That was what he smelled of. Not the shower gel she had found that first day, but fresh pine. Like the woods and nature and the earth itself.

'So, does that mean I can take you out for dinner this week? For a proper date?'

She opened her eyes while the question rolled around in her head. A proper date. Time with just her and Duncan. It sounded ideal, but then she knew this feeling in the pit of her stomach. She was falling, hard. Did she really want to set herself up for possible heartbreak?

'Technically,' she said, 'we already went on a date tonight.'

'What are you on about? We went for dinner with friends.'

'Two couples, not yet together – clearly a double date,' she teased.

'You're a nightmare, you know that?'

'But I'm a nightmare you like,' she replied.

They were close now, so close she could feel the warmth

radiating from him. Her body shifted forwards, desperate to close the space between them, to feel his touch again.

The castle was in sight, but Bex was only half-focused on getting home. She wasn't sure when his hand had slipped into hers, but it felt as natural and easy as anything. Just like the way his other hand rested on the base of her spine, holding her there. Holding her close to him.

'So, if this was a date,' he asked, 'do I get to kiss you goodnight?'

'I don't kiss on the first date,' she whispered back.

'I thought you said it was our second,' he replied, eyebrow raised, a smirk playing at his lips. 'After the shooting and everything.'

'Fine,' she said, trying to hide a smile. 'Then maybe you'll get your kiss on the third.'

'In that case, I'm not taking no for an answer. Wednesday night, The Haven.'

Every rational part of her brain told her this was a bad idea, but the butterflies in her stomach wouldn't let her say no.

'Okay. Wednesday night at The Haven. I'll be there.' Not that she had any idea where that was. She didn't recognise the name, but at that moment she couldn't have cared less. Her mind had lost the ability to string thoughts together properly.

'I'm looking forward to it more than you can imagine,' he said, tilting his head to the side and kissing her gently on the cheek, before turning around and continuing towards the castle. 'Until Wednesday, Barker. Until Wednesday.'

38

As Bex opened the front door to the castle, she let out a breath – she'd actually agreed to go on a date with Duncan. She'd done it. But it was just one date, she reasoned with herself. There was no reason for hearts to get involved. Yet the way hers was thudding against her ribs, it was hard to believe that.

She clicked the door shut behind her, only to startle as a shadow moved in the hallway.

'Ruby,' she said as the dog trotted towards her. 'What are you still doing up? I thought you'd be in bed with Fergus by now.'

'Aye, she would be, but we've been waiting up for you,' came a voice from the drawing room.

Bex followed Ruby to find Fergus sitting in his armchair, the blanket over his lap and a fire burning brightly. As she stood there, she couldn't help but think how he seemed older whenever she saw him in this room. It was so different to when he was out on the grounds or walking up to the village. Then he appeared so sprightly, pacing about with his dogs. Tonight he had even got the fire burning, despite it being summer. Of course she knew that older people felt the cold more, but this was close to stifling.

'I didn't expect you to wait up for me,' she said, perching on the edge of the sofa.

'Well, she was haverin',' he said, with a nod down to Ruby. 'Could nae settle, so I thought I'd come down for a bit and ended up trying one of those coffees you brought. No idea what's in them, but I'm fair buzzing now. Probably won't sleep for a week, so thank you for that.'

Bex felt a smile rise to her lips. Everyone was right – Fergus really was all bark, no bite, and since their drink, or rather drinks, the other weekend, the bark had all but gone.

'I take it you had a good night?' Fergus asked.

'I did, thank you,' she replied. 'Really... braw? Is that how you say it?'

'Kind o', lass. You'll get there.' The old man let out a laugh that turned into a coughing fit. As he leaned forward, Bex moved to fetch him some water, but he lifted his hand and waved for her to stop. 'I'll be 'right. Just give me a wee minute.'

Just as he said, a moment later, his throat had cleared, and he was taking another sip of his whisky.

'I thought I heard young Duncan's voice just now,' he said.

'Yes.' Bex tried to keep her voice as neutral as possible. It was one thing to have Lorna keeping an eye on her; having Fergus do it too was quite another. 'We just walked back together. We were out with some friends – Eilidh and Niall. Lorna couldn't make it, unfortunately, but she was supposed to be there, too.'

'Ah, you've made yourself a good group there,' he said, nodding. 'You seem to have settled in well.'

It was Bex's turn to nod. It was strange to think of herself as 'settling in' to the village. That had been the last thing she'd planned on doing when she'd come up here. But now she had been here a little under two weeks and still had well over a month of work left to do. She was grateful those weeks wouldn't be spent just missing home. If anything, she might actually find herself missing a few people when she returned. And not just people, she thought as she looked down at the red mound by her feet.

'You're a good lass,' Fergus continued. 'Hard worker, that's for sure. But when folk around here let someone in, well, it's no' always easy if things go wrong.'

By folk, Bex got the feeling that Fergus was talking about one person in particular. The one she would miss most of all when it was time for her to go. Still, she offered the laird a relaxed smile.

'I've got that,' she said. 'I know how good the people here are.'

Again, all the subtext was hidden beneath her words.

'Aye, I'm sure you do. And it's you I'm thinking of here, not just them, you know. Take care of yourself, that's all I'll say.'

'Of course, of course,' she replied. 'Besides, I'm pretty tough. You don't need to worry about me.'

Rather than replying, Fergus's gaze shifted to the fireplace and a long sigh billowed from his lips.

'That's what they all say here,' he replied quietly. 'But sometimes it's the toughest one that breaks the hardest.'

Bex got the feeling he was no longer talking about her and Duncan.

39

Bex knew she'd have to tell Claire and Daisy about the date eventually, but when Sunday evening rolled around and they had their normal weekend catch-up, she couldn't bring herself to do it. Instead, she filled them in on everything else she could think of.

'So, Eilidh is a textile artist,' she said, directing the comment to Daisy. 'I haven't seen anything she's done yet, but Niall and Lorna say it's incredible. And I've shown her your paintings. You know, I really think you should come up here before I leave, so you can do some watercolours of the place. There are loads of rooms. I'm sure I could ask Fergus. They have lots of people here when his nephew Kieron runs shoots.'

'Well, if we do come up, it would mean we'd get a chance to meet this burly groundskeeper of yours, so I'm all for it,' Claire replied.

Bex tried to look as casual as possible.

'Sure, I mean, Duncan'll more than likely be at the pub one evening,' she said, trying to sound offhand. 'You'll probably get to meet him then.'

'You're honestly telling us that's it?' Daisy said, her eyebrows raised. 'This is the guy who even had lunch delivered to you when he couldn't make it. You can't tell me you've grown bored of him already?'

A flutter of hope lit in Bex. Apparently, some good came from being the woman who always grew bored with guys at a record pace; she could use it to her advantage now.

'I'll be honest, I don't know how I ever envision myself with someone who spends their entire time outside,' she said. 'I mean, he's hot and everything. But he literally smells like the forest.'

The way she said that, like it was a bad thing, made her chest hurt. She loved the way Duncan smelled of the woods, of nature. Just thinking about it reminded her of the way he had held her on Friday night, with his hand at the base of her spine as he had tucked that strand of hair behind her ear. How was she making out to her best friends in the world that this was nothing, when it was pretty much all she could think about?

'Well, I'm sure there are plenty of other hot Scottish men out there,' Daisy said. 'Maybe we'll see if we can find you one if we come up.'

'That sounds like a plan,' Bex replied, grateful that they had bought her act, even if she was going to have to confess she had kept things about Duncan hidden at a later date.

As Wednesday night drew closer, Bex found herself a mess of thoughts. She already knew Duncan was feeling the same things towards her as she was to him, and the date would likely cement that, but then again, maybe it would be better if the evening was a disaster – if everything went badly, she'd never have the desire to spend any more one-on-one time with him, which in some respects would be ideal. But somehow, she didn't expect that to happen.

The first thing she had to do was work out where the hell The Haven was. A quick google showed her that it was a very fancy hotel around a half a mile outside of the village, which led to the second question of how she was going to get there. Not drinking was out of the question. She was going to need at least two glasses of wine to quash the nerves, but she wouldn't want to drive back, which meant finding a taxi.

After discovering that LochDarroch had nothing in the way of a taxi service, she decided that was probably something a posh hotel would be able to sort, which meant the only thing she had to figure out was her outfit.

More than once, she considered sending her options to the girls, but then that would mean having to admit what was going on, and she wasn't ready to do that. And it wasn't like she didn't have a couple of nice – date-like – outfits, but they were London dates. Swanky cocktail bars. Dinner and a show. They weren't LochDarroch dates.

Still, after trying on every single item from her wardrobe, she decided on a low-back black mini dress that was utterly unsuitable for life in the Highlands. But Duncan had said he liked her as she was, so why shouldn't he see what a date with Rebecca Barker would be like south of the border?

'Sorry, girl, no belly rubs in this,' Bex said as she came down the stairs before her date to find Ruby sitting there, having just been fed. 'You'll rub up against me like you always do, and I know how tricky your fur is to get out of things.'

'You're lookin' very fancy. Off somewhere nice?'

She looked up from Ruby to find Fergus looking directly at her. A lump filled her throat. She didn't have to tell him where she was going. He was her employer-slash-temporary landlord, that was it. But she didn't want to lie to him either.

'Duncan's taking me for dinner at The Haven.'

'Is that right?' His lips twisted together, and Bex couldn't ignore the tension that was weaving its way around between them. 'Well, I'll no' keep you, but any chance you'll take a wee more advice fae an old man?'

Bex nodded, suddenly unable to speak.

'That lad wears his heart on his sleeves. There's no' a bad bone in him, and for one who's been through what he's been through, that says a lot. Just make sure you don't hurt him. That's all I'm asking. He deserves more than that.'

'I know,' she said, then before she realised what she was doing, she walked forward and kissed the old man gently on his cheek. 'Don't worry, I'm not planning on breaking anyone's heart.'

And that included her own.

40

As Bex stepped outside, she pulled her car keys from her bag, only to stop in her tracks. There, on the driveway, was a sleek black sports car, and standing in front of it, dressed in a light green-blue shirt that perfectly matched the colour of his eyes, was Duncan.

'You didn't think you were going to have to drive yourself, did you?' he said, stepping forward and kissing her on the cheek. Somehow, he felt broader than normal. Like if he would wrap his arms around her, she would simply disappear. And yet before there was any chance of that happening, he stepped back and cast her a much longer gaze.

'You look incredible,' he said.

'You don't look bad yourself.'

'Maybe... but you...' It was as though he couldn't hear her. Like he was totally absorbed by what he had seen. Totally absorbed by her. For a moment the pair of them stood there in silence, the weight of his gaze causing her to shudder as her pulse continued to rise.

'I thought we had a reservation we needed to get to,' she said, breaking the tension as she moved towards the car. A moment later, Duncan had regained his focus and was opening the door for her.

'So, whose car is this?' Bex asked as they drove towards the village. 'I feel like it doesn't have enough mud on to be yours.'

'Wow, that's rude,' he said, before he offered her a quick grin to show he was only joking. 'Technically, it's Ishbel's.'

'Ishbel.' It took her a moment to remember where she'd heard that name before. 'Fergus's sister.'

'Aye. Fab woman. She loves her cars, but doesn't have the room for them in London, so she keeps a couple up here.'

'And she's fine with you driving them?'

'As long as Kieron doesn't find out,' he said with a chuckle. 'He can be funny about stuff like that. You know, with me being "help" and everything. Ishbel's not like that though. Last time I saw her she was saying how much like his dad he was, and Ishbel's been divorced these last fifteen years, so it wasn't a compliment.'

Poor Kieron, Bex thought. It seemed like people here didn't think too highly of him, but if he'd grown up in London, he probably found it difficult to understand how things worked around here. She knew she did.

Given that she had already looked up The Haven Hotel online, Bex thought she knew what to expect as they drove down the country lane. But as she stepped inside the building, she felt her breath hitch.

'This is beautiful,' she murmured.

'So, does it meet your London expectations?' Duncan asked, holding out an arm for her to take.

'Absolutely.'

As they strode in through the hallways, where light from crystal chandeliers was reflected in gilded mirrors, Bex struggled to know what to look at next. Unlike the castle, everything here was modern. Sleek and stylish, and yet somehow still fitting with the authenticity of the place.

'They've done really well here,' Duncan said. 'I wouldn't have expected a high-end restaurant in the middle of nowhere, but it's become a bit of a destination spot for food bloggers.'

'Bloggers?' Bex arched an eyebrow.

'Isn't that still what they call people who take photos of everything?' Duncan said.

'I think "bloggers" is a bit 2010 – we're onto influencers now.' She laughed.

'Right. Influencers,' he replied, straightening his shirt as if brushing out invisible creases, although his entire outfit was pristinely ironed. It was almost as if he was nervous.

'Hey, Dunc.' The maître d' stepped forward.

When it became clear she was going to greet Duncan with more than just a 'hello', Bex stepped back, giving her room to kiss him lightly on the cheeks. Both sides, and lingering too. Bex might have been wrong, but she was pretty sure she saw her sigh a little too when they broke apart.

'Hey, Liz, I've booked the table in the corner,' he said, immediately reaching out to take Bex's arm again.

'The best view? Must be a special night,' she said, offering Bex a look, which could have been a smirk, or it could have had a different meaning. Still, Bex smiled politely, before letting Duncan lead her to her seat.

'So, is this a place you come often?' she asked as Duncan pulled out her chair.

'Aye. I try to come by whenever they change the menu,' he said. 'The chef was an old friend of my ma's, so they let me know when there's something new. She sometimes gets me to do tasting when they're trying something a bit more adventurous.'

'Sounds like a dream job, sampling luxury food.'

'It's a good gig.' He grinned. 'They're a nice bunch.'

'Well, they seem very intrigued by your current visit.'

Bex nodded towards the bar, where the maître d' was whispering to the bar staff. All three of them were throwing less than subtle glances over towards the couple.

'Yes, I suppose nobody expected me back here with anyone so soon,' he said before biting down on his lips. 'I might as well tell you know, but this is where Katty had wanted to have the wedding reception.'

'Not the castle?' Bex said, more surprised by that than how Duncan had brought her to his planned wedding venue as a first date. She had seen enough of LochDarroch to know there probably weren't many places like this about, and he clearly wanted to make a good impression.

His eyes glinted with a smile. 'That was what I wanted, but she thought it was a bit dated and dusty. Not to mention not special enough, given that I practically live there and everything.'

She scoffed. How the hell someone could think that the castle wasn't special was beyond her.

'Don't take this the wrong way, but I'm starting to think you got a lucky escape with her.'

'Yeah, I have to admit, things are definitely looking far brighter now,' he said, locking his eyes on hers. His hand was lying flat on the table and Bex found herself desperate to feel their fingers interlocked again, the way they had done on the walk back from the pub. The pub where she had told him he couldn't kiss her. That he would have to wait for another date. This one.

'We should look at the menu,' she said, swallowing back the heat that was threatening to colour her cheeks.

'We should,' he said, but neither of them moved. Despite the fact they weren't even touching, the static had returned with such a force that Bex felt like her whole body might combust if she didn't do something about it soon. Her heart was pounding and from the way his eyes were locked on hers, she was sure he was feeling it too. She was going to place her hand on his. That was what she was going to do. After all, it was only a small gesture.

Her fingers twitched, as if begging to move, and she lifted her arm ever so slightly, wondering why the hell she was feeling so damn nervous, when there was a slight cough to her side. Bex turned her head to see a waiter smiling broadly at the pair.

'So, can I get some drinks for you?'

Perfect timing, she thought, and just like that, the moment was gone.

41

Bex couldn't remember ever being on a date with someone who genuinely wanted to learn so much about her. London men weren't like that. Or at least the ones she'd dated weren't. They wanted to tell you about themselves – the deals they'd made, the places they'd holidayed, the celebrities they'd met. They'd ask questions occasionally, but it was usually just to set up another chance to talk about their own lives.

'So, you've got a brother, right? And your mum and dad – are they still together?'

'Oh, yes,' Bex said with a sigh. 'My parents are the perfect couple. Totally in love, even after all their years together. It's sickening. I sort of blame them for my hopelessness with relationships.'

'Really? Why?'

'It's hard to live up to something like that. I'm always looking for a partnership that's like theirs. Relationships should be partnerships, don't you think?'

'Absolutely,' he agreed.

'The thing is, most guys say that, but living it is a different matter. I don't want to give up my work, but that intimidates a lot of men, especially since I tend to earn more than they do.'

Duncan arched an eyebrow, widening those perfectly swimmable eyes.

'Well, you definitely earn more than me, that's for sure. I don't think Fergus has given me a pay rise in seven years.'

'What?' Bex's eyes widened. 'That's not okay. You need to talk to him about that.'

Duncan chuckled. 'There's no point, honestly. I don't pay for anything at the lodge, and to rent a place like that – with bills, water... it's worth a lot.'

'I guess.'

'He also covers the car, petrol, and even tabs at the pubs. I probably have a lot more savings and disposable income than most people my age. Or at least I did until I bought the ring.'

The mood around the table shifted slightly.

'You don't feel like you could sell it?' Bex said, the words an unwanted reminder that dating Duncan on any level was a bad idea. But it wasn't like there was anything she could do about it now.

'In order to do that, she would have had to have given it back to me.'

'She didn't give it back?' Bex blurted out, feeling a jolt of shock.

'Not yet,' he said with a slight shrug. 'To be fair, I haven't asked for it.'

'You need to. She can't just hold on to that after what she did.'

'You're starting to sound like Lorna.'

'Well, that's just because Lorna cares about you, too.'

His smile twisted. 'Are you saying you care about me?'

He'd backed her into a corner, and she knew it. And so much

for thinking the mood had dropped. That damn static was back in the air, sending tingles through every part of her.

'Well, you've helped me a lot,' Bex said, trying to replicate the same casual shrug he'd managed while talking about the engagement ring. 'You've probably saved me over a week of work.'

'Which I regret, actually,' he said, the slightest smirk twisting on his lips. 'If I'd known, I would've made an absolute mess of things just to make sure you'd have to stay longer.'

There it was again, that electric charge between them. Bex felt her whole body ignite as if drawn to him by an invisible force.

'I really want to kiss you,' Duncan said softly. 'Would that be okay? If I kissed you?'

Every ounce of common sense she had was telling her to say no. They could still leave tonight without kissing, having had an amazing night. They could be flirty friends. That would be okay. And yet he had asked her if he could kiss her. Who the hell did that?

Before she could find her voice, Bex felt her chin dip, almost as if her body was answering for her.

'I think I'd like that too,' she whispered.

A second later, he leaned across the table and pressed his lips to hers.

It was an explosion of fireworks. It felt like the kiss she'd been waiting for her entire life – the one that set her whole body alight. As she pressed herself closer to him, his fingers found the back of her neck, holding her with a gentle nervousness, as if he feared she might suddenly change her mind and back away from him. But there was no chance of that happening.

'Your first course?'

Bex felt her cheeks burn as the pair broke away and she saw

the waiter standing there, two plates in his hands. Wordlessly, he placed them down.

'Enjoy,' he said before disappearing.

'I swear they did that deliberately,' Duncan muttered.

Bex didn't even glance at whatever it was she had been brought. Instead, her eyes were locked on Duncan. While he hadn't gone the same fluorescent red she was sure she had gone, there was a definite pink to his ears, though it did little to distract from his ear-to-ear grin. A grin that, judging from the ache in her cheeks, she was mirroring.

'Well, that was something,' she managed.

'I'd say it was worth the wait for the third date.'

'Maybe,' she said, though it was difficult to play it coy when her heart was pounding hard enough to burst out her ribcage.

'So we should eat,' he said, still not having broken eye contact since the moment their kiss ended.

'We should,' she replied, and then, because the smell was divine and she was well aware they could be stuck in the same position all night if one of them didn't move, she picked up her knife and fork and began to eat.

For a second, she kept her eyes on the plate, sensing that Duncan was still looking at her, when finally he let out a light chuckle.

'What the hell are you doing to me, Barker?' he said.

There was no denying it. That kiss had confirmed everything she feared. Bex was in trouble. She was falling for the groundskeeper. Hard.

42

The food was exceptional. It was one of those places that served barely a mouthful per course, and Bex had to force herself to take miniature forkfuls, so she didn't simply devour the tiny little mousse in one. Though, as delicious as it was, the food was far from what occupied Bex's thoughts. Instead, she found herself waiting for the moment when the waiter would come and take their plates away, so she and Duncan could kiss again without the risk of trailing her hair in the jus or sabayon, or whatever type of sauce was drizzled across her plate.

When she finished her first course, her hand met his across the table. Their fingers entwined, steepled together, and with their grip on one another reassuringly firm, Duncan lifted his hand so that he kissed along the line of her knuckles. All the while, his eyes never left hers. The action was far more subtle than any kiss, and yet so intimate it was like the entire world had disappeared and they were the only things that mattered.

Even when he lowered their hands, he shifted his position so that his leg brushed up against hers under the table. And she reciprocated, leaning into him. It was as if they were trying to touch as many places of one another as they could, while still being out in public at a restaurant.

'So, are you having a good night?' he asked. There was no hint of a smirk on his lips. It was a genuine question.

'There have definitely been some high points,' she replied.

'Oh, and what might they be?'

She lifted her gaze, as if she was having to think about the question.

'Well, it's definitely the best wine I've had since I came up here.'

Duncan's laugh was so loud, several people turned to look at them.

'The wine, really?' His eyebrows were so high they butted his headline.

'Well, I normally find dessert the highlight, but we haven't got to that yet.'

'Dessert and wine. Wow, I need to up my game for you, don't I, Barker? How about I get to tell you my favourite things then instead?'

'You mean it's not the wine, too?' Bex joked. The truth was, she was just desperate to hear that laugh again, although the chuckle he responded with was almost as warming. There was something about hearing Duncan laugh that made everything else in the world evaporate.

'No, it's not the wine,' he said. 'That's not even top five.'

'Well, in that case, I need to hear the full top five list.' She grinned.

'Of course you do.' Rather than responding, he pressed his lips tightly together before he looked down at their entwined fingers.

'Well, number five is this,' he said, lifting his hand slightly to show what he was referring to.

'Only number five?' she said, genuinely surprised. The casual way in which they held one another's hands was probably her favourite thing about the evening – other than the kiss, of course. She was desperate to know what could beat that.

'Now I'm intrigued,' she said. 'Number four must be good.'

'Number four is this,' he said, raising his leg ever so slightly and trailing it along the inside of her thigh. A slight gasp escaped her lips, eliciting a perfect knowing smile from Duncan.

'Okay, that's a good number four,' she agreed, trying to lessen the pounding in her chest – though how she was going to do that, she had no idea. There were still three more things left on his list.

'Number three. When I first saw you coming up to the castle.' His expression was a picture of sincerity. 'You took my breath away, Barker. I really didn't know that was possible. I thought it was just an expression, but somehow you did it.'

She bit down on her lower lip, her body desperate to be closer to him. To kiss him again. But she was also desperate to hear what the other things were.

'Okay, so what about the top two?'

'Well, number two has to be the kiss, doesn't it? No doubt about that.'

'Number two?' she echoed. 'What's number one? And don't you dare say food or wine.'

'No, number one is this.' He released her hand before slowly lifting his and brushing his thumb gently along her jawline. As if on instinct, her eyes involuntarily closed. His thumb continued to move, this time along her bottom lip. With her pulse hammering so hard she could barely hear, Bex tried to stifle a second gasp, but it was impossible. As the sound escaped, Duncan's hand moved again, this time to cradle the back of her neck as he whispered into her ear.

'You are incredible.'

The warmth from his breath sent shivers down her spine. And then, for the second time, his lips pressed against hers.

She wouldn't have thought it possible, but somehow the kiss was even more electric than the first one. Whether it had been the anticipation, the waiting for it, or just the fact that with every touch he knew her body more and more, she didn't know. But when she broke away, she found her eyes were still closed.

'Well,' she said when she opened them again. 'That list fails on two points, I'm afraid.'

His laugh was deep and resonant. Everything she hoped it would be.

'Why? You said I shouldn't mention food, and I didn't.'

'I know, but it had to be based on things that had already happened. And your little trick with your leg, not to mention that kiss, hadn't happened when you started your list. So I'm afraid your top five is null and void.'

He shook his head, laughter still rolling from him.

'Well, it probably should be. I lied anyway.'

'You did?'

'Yeah. My number one wasn't even on there.'

'Really, so what was it?' she asked, ready for whatever cocky remark he was about to give. Instead, he took her hand again.

'Talking to you. Getting to know you. That's it. That's been the best bit. Even without all the other bits. Without the kiss, or the holding hands, it's been the best night I can remember having in a long time. No, scrap that actually,' he said, correcting himself. 'Ever. I can't ever remember having a night like this.'

She wanted to tell him he was being ridiculous. Soppy. Or maybe he was just great at playing her, but she didn't think that was the case. She may not know him well, but you didn't get such loyal friends as he had by being a player.

'But,' he said, sitting up straight and picking up his wine, 'the dessert is really good, so maybe I should wait until we've had that before we make a concrete list.'

Bex shook her head, wishing he didn't make her laugh quite so much. 'Maybe you should,' she agreed. 'Dessert is normally my highlight, after all.'

43

The dessert was mouth-wateringly good, but even so, it didn't come close to Bex's number one spot of the night, though it was hard to know what had. At some point, their chairs had shifted around the table so that they no longer had to lean across it to kiss one another, and it felt like any second Duncan's hands weren't occupied with cutlery, they were touching her. Touching her legs, stroking her arm, running his fingertip in lazy circles across her palm. Bex had heard of people talking about their love languages before, but she never really thought about it too deeply; yet now, if she was asked, she would have to say that Duncan's was touch. And judging from the way her body reacted to him, hers was too.

He was busy stroking the top of her thigh with the back of his hand when his phone buzzed. He pulled it out of his pocket and glanced at the screen.

'So, our taxi is waiting outside,' he said.

'Taxi? You already sorted one?' Somewhere between the first kiss and now, Bex had totally forgotten that she needed to find a way to get home, but thankfully, Duncan seemed to have the issue sorted. Although when, she had no idea. He hadn't left the table, or her side, all night.

'Sort of. It's pretty difficult to get one here, so I just pulled in a favour instead.'

'Well, now I'm intrigued,' she replied, gently pressing another kiss against his lips.

'Just don't set your expectations too high, all right?'

Bex backed away, her eyes wide. 'After this evening? I should probably tell you now that if there's not a limo waiting outside, then this entire night's going to be bust.'

The first hints of a grin formed on Duncan's face. 'The entire night? Does that mean it's already over?' he said, kissing her again.

'Well, let me see how bad this taxi is before I make up my mind.'

'Sounds fair enough,' he said.

Duncan's 'taxi' turned out to be a Land Rover, driven by none other than Roddy.

'Ma'am, we meet again,' Roddy said, tipping his head as Bex approached.

She couldn't help but arch an eyebrow. 'Roddy, I don't know what I may have done to make you think I'm old enough to be referred to as a ma'am, but please, never do it again.'

'Aye, gotcha,' Roddy said, quickly backing up towards the driver's seat.

'Do you want to sit in the front or back?' Duncan said, reaching to open the car door.

Bex paused. What she actually wanted was to sit beside him. She wanted her body to be as close to him as possible. After the last hour, the thought of not being able to touch him caused a deep throb to ache in her chest. But she was being ridiculous. It was just the wine talking, that was all. Not that they'd had that much. One bottle between the pair of them throughout the entire meal. They'd been too busy talking and kissing to manage more than that. However, not wanting to seem crazy, she simply said, 'I'm fine in the back.'

After helping her up, Duncan slid into the front seat and Roddy started the car as he began asking Duncan questions, mostly about Fergus and the grounds. Bex watched as Duncan tried his best to answer, but he wasn't focusing on Roddy. Instead, he kept glancing back at her, and each look made her stomach flip. This was ludicrous, she thought. Absolutely ludicrous. There was no logical reason for this to work and as far as she could tell, even in the best-case scenario, one of them would come out with a broken heart. But the thought of forgetting about the night, the kisses, the conversation, his damn laugh, just felt impossible.

'Am I dropping you at the castle or the lodge? Or both?' Roddy asked, throwing Duncan a look.

'Umm, I'm not sure. I'm at the lodge.'

A pause slid into the car. One Bex knew she was responsible for filling.

'Well, I wouldn't mind seeing Kenna again,' she said, the grin on her face stretching involuntarily.

Duncan twisted around to look at her, his eyes alight. 'I'm sure she'd love to see you, too. Although, what will Ruby do without you?'

'She might have to spend the night with Fergus and the other dogs.' Even as she spoke, she couldn't help but think she was being crazy, but what was it Fergus had said about making memories? This night definitely felt like one of those.

'To the lodge, please,' Duncan told Roddy.

44

The entire ride, Bex's mind raced with anticipation of what the night would hold and, by the time the lodge came into view, her body was so raw with adrenaline that her legs trembled.

As Duncan opened her car door, she turned and looked at Roddy.

'Thank you ever so much for the lift,' she said.

'No worries.'

'And maybe...' She hesitated. 'Maybe if you see Lorna any time soon, you could keep this to yourself?'

He let out a slight chuckle before lifting his fingers to his lips and making a twisting motion.

'She won't hear a word from me,' he said, at which she flashed a quick smile before stepping out of the car.

As the Land Rover reversed away from the house, Bex turned to Duncan, though rather than the grin she expected to see on his face, a deep frown furrowed his brows.

'What is it?' she said. 'Is everything all right?'

'Everything's great,' he said, offering her a fleeting smile. 'Only...'

'Only?' A flurry of nerves whipped through her as he took hold of her hand and pulled her in close so that her chest was almost pressed against his. His eyes were trained on hers.

'I don't want you to do something you'll regret tonight,' he said.

For a second, Bex assumed he was joking – that this was his attempt at humour – only that frown line of his was still firmly in place.

'Duncan, I have done this before. Quite a few times.'

He let out a small sound. 'I know that. Well, I assumed. But that doesn't change things. Bex, I meant what I said tonight about you. About you being the most incredible woman I've ever met.' He lifted his hand and gently cupped one side of her face. Involuntarily, she felt her weight fall into him. 'I'm crazy about you. And...'

'And I'm leaving,' she said, filling in the blank that he was leaving unsaid. 'It makes things complicated.'

'It does,' he replied.

His fingertips had slipped into her hair now, while his other hand had fallen back into that little dip at the base of her spine, which, at that precise moment, felt like it had been created solely for the purpose of him holding her.

'So where does that leave us?' she asked, wishing she could control the ache spreading through her chest. 'You don't want to do this?'

'Are you kidding?' For the first time since they had stepped out of the car, the frown lines had gone, and in their place was a look of pure disbelief. 'Of course I want to do this. But it doesn't have to be tonight. I can wait. I can wait as long as you want to. And if you decide that it's not worth the risk, the potential heartbreak, then I'll get it. There's no rush here, Barker. I'm yours if you want me. Now, tomorrow, whenever.'

It was quite possibly the sweetest thing a man had ever said to her, although if his purpose had been to put her off him, he had well and truly failed. Instead, she pushed herself up onto her tiptoes and pressed her lips against his. She could feel the tension that ebbed through him, although with every breath she took, a little more of it dissolved. Soon it was as if they were one mass of need. The fear of heartbreak was gone. They weren't going to hurt each other. How could they do that? The thought was absurd. They barely knew each other. This was... Well, she didn't know what it was, but she knew she wasn't going to give it up.

Her hands wandered down his back, where she pulled his shirt out from the top of his trousers and slid her hand up his back. A simultaneous gasp escaped both their lips. That was the first time she had touched him like this – felt her palm against the softness of his skin – and she wanted to see more. Feel more.

'I need to open the door,' Duncan said, drawing sharp breaths between their kisses. 'I need to get you inside. Now.' As he finished talking, a slight shadow of a frown came back in place. 'As long as you want to?' he added.

Bex rolled her eyes. 'I swear, if you ask me that once more, then I'm going up to the castle and I'll never speak to you again.'

'Noted,' he said, grabbing the door handle.

As it clicked open, he turned back around and took Bex's hand to lead her in, yet before he had stepped through the threshold, he stopped. For a second, she feared he was going to ask her again, at which point he might expect her to make good on her promise and go back to the castle, and there was no chance she wanted that to happen. But instead, he dropped to the ground, letting go of Bex's hand as he did.

'Sorry, girl,' Duncan said as he picked up his giant cat from the floor. 'But tonight, you're going to be sleeping out here.'

45

Bex didn't know what time it was, but the birds were beginning their dawn chorus outside. Not that they had woken her. She wasn't even sure she had fallen asleep. At that moment, she was lying with her head on Duncan's chest, rising and falling with the rhythm of his breath. Her mind filled with everything the night had entailed, from the laughter over dinner, to the way his lips had felt as he'd pressed them into the nape of her neck, kissing slowly down, across her collarbone, down her arm all the way to her hand, where he had kissed each finger one at a time, all while never taking his eyes off her.

The night had been everything she could have dreamt of and more. It wasn't just the kisses that were unlike anything she had ever experienced before; it was every physical aspect she experienced with him.

'You should know, I'm actually really nervous,' he'd said as they'd stood in his bedroom. By this point, she had already stripped him of his shirt and belt and was making headway on the buttons of his jeans too, but his words caused her to stop in her tracks.

'You are. Why?'

He cleared his throat, only for that slight pink tinge to colour the top of his ears.

'Katty and I... She was my first... My only.'

Bex tried not to show her surprise. Of course, it made sense that Katty would have been his first. They had been childhood sweethearts, but they had been separated for a couple of months now and she had seen the way women – like the maître d' at the restaurant – looked at him. She had assumed he'd tried to get over his heartbreak the way so many others did, at least a few times. But apparently that wasn't the case.

'Don't worry, I'll be gentle with you.' She smirked.

'Is that right?' He grinned.

'Maybe. I guess you'll just have to wait and see.'

The truth was, it had been perfect. So much so that she could barely feel where her body ended and his began. But the physical side of it was only a fraction of their night. There had been the way he had whispered in her ear that caused every hair on the back of her neck to rise. The way his lips traced the line across her skin and the manner in which his hands fit into the small of her back every time he pulled her closer to him. There was the way they had laughed when his feet got caught in his boxers and the way he'd made it so clear that, if at any point she changed her mind, then that was fine with him. He just wanted her there with him.

Now it was morning, and they lay with arms and legs intertwined as he drew lazy figures of eight on her stomach, her arm, any part of her body he could touch. Not that she was any better. It was damn near impossible to keep her hands off him.

'I should probably go up to the castle,' she said as she stretched out, fully aware of how much of her body was touching his. 'I've got work to get on with.'

'Take a sick day,' he said, his fingers moving up towards her sternum. 'You know, I've heard there's a nasty bug going around. Has people laid up in bed for at least a week. Maybe you're coming down with that. You should stay. Rest.'

She laughed. 'Well, if that's the case, I should probably leave,' she said, sitting up. 'I'd hate for you to get sick too.' Before she was even upright, Duncan had grabbed her by the wrist and pulled her back down.

'I think you're right,' he said, kissing her deeply as if he was trying to taste the very essence of her, before breaking away far too soon. 'I think we should both stay here and quarantine for at least a week. I'll ring Fergus now and let him know.'

Once again, she allowed herself to be devoured by his touch. It was far too tempting to stay there. At least for a couple more hours, but how would that help things? Well, the longer it took her to get her work done at the castle, the longer it would be she stayed in Scotland, but wasn't that the point.

The realisation that this was doomed to fail caused a weight to press down on her chest.

'What is it?' Duncan asked.

'What? What do you mean?' Bex feigned innocence, yet his withering expression said it all, only intensifying the weight inside her. How the hell could he read her so well already?

'I was just thinking about when the job's done. When I have to go back.'

'Right.' Silence swelled through the air before Duncan shifted, moving onto his side and looking straight at her.

'Look,' he said, tucking invisible strands of hair behind her ear. 'I know we don't know what's going to happen in the next couple of months with us, but let's be honest, no one ever does. You might think you know what the future holds. You might have written a plan out for the next five years, but that doesn't mean the universe is going to work that way. It only takes one moment to derail everything you thought was going to happen. Everything you worked towards.'

Bex didn't know if he was talking about him, or her and her set plan towards promotion, but she stayed silent, the air unusually tight in her lungs as he continued.

'So how about this?' he carried on. 'How about we don't plan? We don't imagine what the future is going to be – whether that's the worst-case scenario or the best possible outcome – we just get to love every day we have together. We make the most of each moment. We don't dwell. We don't worry. We're just us, together. How does that sound?'

It sounded perfect. So perfect that Bex tried to smile, but the weight in her chest had now spread to consume her entirety. Everything he did and said made her fall for him more, and she got the feeling he felt the same. Which was why she knew no matter what he said, it was going to be near impossible not to think about what the future would hold for them. But she was sure as hell going to try.

'We just take each day as it comes,' she said, paraphrasing what he'd just said.

'Exactly.' He kissed her again, before breaking away, a wide grin on his face. 'And this one comes with breakfast in bed.'

46

While Duncan disappeared into the kitchen, Bex was joined by his giant Maine Coon, who immediately began nuzzling her head into her, demanding fuss.

'I'm sorry I took him from you last night,' Bex said as she stroked the cat. Several times over the course of the night Bex had heard things clattering in the living room. Duncan had told her before that Kenna's response to being annoyed was to knock things off the shelves, and judging from the sounds, he hadn't been joking. At least once, it sounded like something had broken, but she'd have had to get out of bed to go and check, and that wasn't something she was planning on doing. 'I know how much you love him, but you don't mind sharing him for a little bit, do you?'

The cat's purring intensified.

'He's really great, isn't he? I mean, you already know that, but I'm going to tell you something now, and you have to keep it a secret, right?'

Kenna continued demanding more attention, clearly not

that bothered by Bex's secret as long as she was still getting her fuss, but Bex carried on talking.

'I'm really scared I'm going to break his heart. I don't want to. I really don't want to, but his life is up here and mine is down in London, and I know the best thing to do would be to put this down to a mistake, but I'm not sure I can do that. Is that wrong of me? To want to be with him, even though I'm pretty sure I'm going to hurt him?'

'Everything all right in here?'

Duncan's head appeared in the doorway, causing Bex's pulse to spike, although she was immediately distracted by the large mixing bowl in his hand.

'You're cooking?' Bex asked, praying he hadn't heard what she'd said to his cat, but by the way he was sporting that casual grin of his, she was pretty sure he hadn't.

'Just drop scones. Pancakes. I've put some bacon in. I'm afraid you'll have to wait until the castle to get your decent coffee, though. I've just got instant here.'

'Well, that's something we're going to have to rectify if I'm going to stay here again.'

'Oh, is it?' he said, walking into the room and leaning down to kiss her.

'It is. In fact, lack of decent coffee might be the reason I have to call this whole thing off.'

With a deep laugh, he stood back upright, shaking his head as he continued to whisk his mixture.

'In that case, a coffee machine has just gone to the top of my shopping list.'

As he turned to leave, Bex was about to say that perhaps this time she should be the one to buy the coffee machine, given that he'd already bought one for her. But before she could get a word out, there was a knock at the door.

Her pulse shot up for a second time.

'Who's that?' she asked. 'Are you expecting anyone?'

A vision of Lorna outside and full of rage shot through Bex's mind. Had she heard she was here? Or maybe it was Fergus, horrified by her inappropriate behaviour. Perhaps he had already rung Nigel at the office and told him that instead of staying up in the castle and working like she was meant to be, she was sleeping with the groundskeeper. That would be the end of her career, for sure. Yet despite her panic, Duncan looked completely calm.

'It'll just be Roddy or Horace,' he said. 'Don't worry, I'll get rid of them.'

With Bex's pulse still struggling to recover, Duncan walked out of the bedroom. A moment later, she heard the front door open.

'What the hell do you want?'

Duncan's voice caused a corkscrew of confusion to rip through Bex. She had never heard Duncan speak like that to anyone and given the mood he had been in only seconds ago, she couldn't imagine who the hell would warrant that kind of reaction. And then, all of a sudden, she could.

'Please, I just want to talk.' The response came from a woman's voice. Katty.

'This is not a good time.'

'I need to talk to you,' Katty pleaded, her voice desperate.

Bex was out of the bed now, creeping towards the door, desperate to hear every word that was being said.

'I have nothing to say to you,' Duncan replied. His voice was less sharp than it had been, but there was still an edge to it. 'Whatever you want, I'm not the person to help you with it any more. I'm not yours any more, Katty. You need to leave.'

The way he had said those words about not being Katty's any

more caused a deep throb to build in Bex. She knew what they meant, even if Katty didn't. He was hers now. They were one another's.

'Please,' Katty said, taking a shaky breath. 'Please, Duncan, I have to talk to you.'

'This really isn't—'

'I'm pregnant, Duncan.'

47

Bex was scrambling for clothes. They didn't even need to be hers. Instead, she picked up Duncan's jeans and shirt from last night and slung them on. Then, picking up her heels, she stumbled out of the room and into the front of the house, where Duncan and Katty were standing.

The woman's eyes widened at the sight of Bex, but she said nothing. Unlike Duncan.

'Bex, don't go,' he pleaded. 'Please, wait. I just need... I just have to...'

He couldn't finish his sentence. Of course he couldn't. What was he going to say to her? His childhood sweetheart was there, and she was having his baby. Whatever had happened between them didn't matter.

'I have to get to work,' she said, pushing past them both, barely hearing Duncan calling after her. Her head was spinning. Katty was pregnant. That was what she'd just heard. Katty was pregnant.

As she clutched the waistband of Duncan's jeans, her bare feet stinging on the stone paths, she didn't know if she should laugh or cry. So much for what she'd said to Kenna about being the one to hurt Duncan. She couldn't have got that more wrong if she'd tried. The way her heart clenched, as if being pierced by Katty's perfectly manicured nails, was all the evidence she needed. She had fallen for the groundskeeper, and he was having a baby with another woman.

She fumbled through the castle's front door, her vision blurred by hot, stinging tears that caused her to trip straight over the bounding red mound in front of her.

'For crying out loud!' she snapped, only for the guilt to roll through her. She knelt done on the cold stone floor. 'I'm sorry, Ruby,' she said, rubbing the dog's head. 'I'm so sorry, girl. I didn't mean to shout like that. It's just been a bad morning. A really bad morning.'

'Everything all right?' Fergus appeared in the hallway, a blanket wrapped around his shoulders. 'Guessing the night wasn't quite the success you'd hoped.' His voice was soft and Bex tried to laugh, but the attempt only made the tears spill faster. She quickly wiped them away, trying to compose herself.

'I was just going to use that machine o' yours to make a coffee,' Fergus continued. 'Not sure I got it right last time. I was hoping you'd show me how it works? You look like you could do with one yourself. Can add a dash of whisky in it too. I normally do.'

Bex wanted nothing more than to hide under the covers and cry until she fell asleep. But something about the way Fergus looked at her told her this wasn't the kind of offer you turned down.

'Okay,' she said quietly.

While she fixed the coffees, Fergus retrieved a bottle of something dark from the back of one of the cupboards and added a small splash to their mugs. Whatever it was, it warmed her throat and spread comfortingly through her chest.

'Sorry things didn't go as you'd hoped,' he said. 'If it was Duncan's fault, I'll—'

'No, no, it wasn't Duncan's fault,' she interrupted. 'Not at all. Duncan's a perfect gentleman, which I guess makes it even worse. It's just... complicated.' As much as she was desperate to unload, she knew it wasn't her place to tell Fergus about Duncan and the baby.

'Grown-up relationships often are,' he replied with a faint smile. 'Although, Winny and I weren't. Not really.'

Bex was curious and seized on the chance for a distraction from her own sorry state.

'Do you miss her?'

He chuckled, then took a sip of his drink. 'She was nice. A lovely woman. But she didn't set my heart on fire the way I suspect young Duncan does for you. And you for him, from what he said.'

'He spoke about me?' Bex asked in surprise.

'Aye, a little.'

She wasn't sure if that should make her feel pleased or not. Right now, her heart felt like a pile of smouldering ashes, rather than anything remotely on fire.

'Did you ever have someone like that?' she asked, eager to shift the conversation from her own heartache. She remembered the photograph of Fergus and Duncan's grandfather in the study, and a young woman in between them. 'Someone who set the whole world alight for you?'

Fergus's gaze drifted off into the past, his face softened by memories.

'Aye, I did. She lit up my world.'

'What happened?' Bex asked, her voice hushed.

'She got sick.' He sighed deeply, pain flickering in his eyes. 'We thought it was just a bug. Something she'd shake off. She told me she'd see the doctor, get it sorted, and that was the last time I saw her. Her family came to tell me the doctors found somethin', and she'd gone away to get treatment. I thought when she came back, I'd propose. Got the ring and everything, but...'

'But she didn't come back,' Bex whispered.

He nodded. 'No. After that, I dinnae want to marry anyone else. But, with a place like this, there were expectations. Ishbel was the one who introduced me to Winny. And my sister's got a good read on folk, most of the time anyway. And she was right about that match. Winny an' I had good years together. She was my best friend, and in lots of ways, that's all you can hope for.'

Bex nodded, suddenly feeling as if her own heartache paled in comparison. Her feelings for Duncan, whatever they were, would heal with time. But Fergus had lost something irreplaceable.

As she thought of the old man, she remembered the notebook she had found, with the names of all the different hospitals. Was that to do with this love of his life? She was inclined to think it was.

'Let me give you a piece of advice from an old man,' Fergus said, studying her intently. 'Just keep living. We've only got one life, and maybe if I'd lived a little more, opened my heart a bit more, I would've made more of it. Just keep living, all right?'

'I will,' she said, managing a slight smile before she took a long sip of her coffee. 'I should get dressed,' she said, looking down at her attire. 'And then get to work. Lots to do.'

'You know what?' Fergus said, a slanted smile rising on his lips. 'You should take a day off. I think you've earned it. And I promise I won't tell your boss.'

48

The first thing Bex did on her day off was talk to the girls. It was the first time in ages she'd had them both on a video call, and though she'd wanted to appear completely fine and okay, the second they came onto the screen, the tears started tumbling down her cheeks.

'What the hell happened?' Daisy said, concern flooding her voice.

'Oh, nothing, nothing. Just... Duncan and I... we... we...'

There was no way she could keep it from them any longer, and so she didn't. She told them everything, from the near kiss on the way back from the pub, to the date and the night at his place, and then to the final bit. Katty's appearance.

'What?' Claire gasped.

'Oh God, I'm so sorry,' Daisy added.

'It's crap. It really is,' Bex said, wiping at her eyes, 'but what's stupid is, I actually hurt for him, almost as much as for myself. Maybe even a bit more.'

'What? Why?'

'Because I know he doesn't want to be with her. He doesn't.

But I know he's going to do the right thing. That's the type of person he is. It doesn't matter that he doesn't love her, he's going to go back to her. He's going to be with her and the baby.'

'Jesus, that's tough,' Daisy said, shaking her head.

'Yeah, that's one way of putting it...'

Even now, all Bex could think about was Duncan and this relationship he'd be stuck in. He'd told her he and Katty were drifting apart, that they wanted different things, and she'd known he wasn't lying. Just like the way she'd known he wasn't lying when they'd been curled up together on his bed and he'd said how he'd never expected to feel anything like what he felt with her. But now he and Katty would be forced together out of a sense of obligation. Both trapped in lives that neither of them really wanted.

'So what are you going to do?' Claire asked. 'I mean, you don't have to see him, do you?'

'He doesn't live at the castle, just on the castle grounds, but no, you're right. I don't have to see him. Actually, I was thinking about just taking everything home to sort. All the ledgers and things. Now that I've got it organised, I could do a lot of my work at my flat.'

'Well, why not do that?'

Bex thought about it. She'd considered it when she first arrived at the castle. If she could get the ledgers to fit in the back of her car, she could drive back to London and start sorting it in the comfort of her own home. It would likely take more than one trip, but that was hardly the end of the world. She could head home with half of it now and come back for the rest in a few weeks. Give herself time to get Duncan out of her system, so to speak.

'It's something to think about,' she said. 'Today, I'm just taking it easy. Fergus has given me the day off.'

'In the middle of the week?' Daisy asked, eyebrows raised.

'Well... I kind of stumbled in in tears this morning,' she admitted, smiling a little. 'I think he was worried he'd have to deal with me crying all day if I was working.'

'I'm sure that's not it,' Daisy replied, but the look on her face said otherwise.

'What are you going to do, then?' Claire asked.

'Not much. Just take a walk to the village, clear my head. Get a pub lunch.'

'That sounds nice. Just stay in touch, won't you?'

Bex was about to assure them she would when her phone buzzed with a new message. She glanced down and saw it was from Duncan.

'What is it?' Claire asked, noticing the sudden flicker of emotion on Bex's face. 'Is everything all right?'

'Everything's fine,' Bex said, sweeping her finger across the message to delete it without even reading it. Whatever it said, it wouldn't make things better. She knew that. Right now, she needed to get Duncan out of her mind and that meant forgetting he even existed.

49

It was warmer than Bex expected as she walked. Or maybe it was simply the pace she'd set that made her so hot. She crossed the castle grounds and headed towards the loch, her eyes fixed forward, careful not to glance in the direction of the lodge. There would have been tears, she thought. Lots of apologies. Promises that things would be okay. Lies they knew they had to say to one another because their lives were changed forever now. They were going to be parents.

As she wiped the tears from her cheeks, she wondered how it was possible that she still had any left. This wasn't the first time she'd cried over a man, but all those other times it had felt like something she needed to do to get them out of her system. And half the time it hadn't been about them anyway. It had been about her. Her failure to find that happy ever after that she dreamt of. Her failure to find someone who thought of her as theirs and theirs alone. But Duncan had thought that, hadn't he? After only two weeks knowing each other and one night together, he had said those words to Katty. 'I'm not yours any more.' That's what he'd said. But words meant nothing. Not now.

By the time she reached the pub, it was three o'clock in the afternoon and she was sweaty and hot. Even though she wasn't particularly hungry, she knew better than not to eat anything. And so she headed to the Lion, wanting nothing more than to hide herself away, but when she walked in, she realised her mistake. There, standing behind the bar, doing one of her countless jobs, was Lorna.

The redhead's eyes lit up at the sight of Bex and before she realised what was happening, Lorna was out from the bar, squeezing her in a hug.

'So?' Lorna said when she broke away. 'I believe you've got something you need to tell me? Something about my brother.'

Bex froze, wondering if Lorna already knew about the pregnancy.

'Liz rang me last night,' Lorna said, giving her a wink. 'She said you and Duncan were all over each other at The Haven. I mean, I should be mad. I am mad, but from what Eilidh said after you four had dinner, apparently it was inevitable. According to her, you two were sneaking glances at each other the entire night, and he offered to walk you home… She also said Duncan was the happiest she had seen him since… well ever, really. And I'm guessing that's down to you. So I take back what I said before. You have my blessing to date my brother, for what it's worth. Not that it stopped you before.'

Lorna's smile was genuine, her happiness clear. She approved of them, was actually happy about it, and now Bex had to crush that happiness.

'It's not quite that straightforward,' Bex said hesitantly.

'Why? What happened?'

'I'm not sure it's my place to tell you.'

Bex didn't want to break down again. She had only just got a grip of her tears and the last thing she wanted was to turn into a blubbering wreck in the middle of the pub, even if it was on a Wednesday afternoon. But she could feel her eyes welling and her breaths growing shallower, and she already knew there was nothing she could do about it.

'Bex?' Lorna's eyes narrowed. 'Either you tell me what happened right now, or I'll march right over to my brother's house and kick his arse for making you look like that. So, which is it going to be?'

50

Five minutes later, Lorna was no longer behind the bar, but sitting at one of the tables with a large whisky in front of her.

'No, no way. There is no way that I can possibly be related to the spawn of Katty McLeod.'

Given that Lorna and Duncan were stepsiblings, she and the baby wouldn't actually be blood relations, Bex thought, but she didn't think it was a good idea to bring that up. Not considering how truly horrified Lorna was by this news.

'Have you spoken to him?'

'No, not since I left there this morning. The last thing he needs is me complicating the situation right now. He's obviously got a lot going on.'

'You see, this is why you're perfect for him – because you actually think about what is best for him. She never did that. Ever.'

Bex wasn't sure whether being described as 'perfect for him' should have made her feel good, but all it did was cause a knot to twist in her stomach.

'He'll do the right thing, won't he?' Bex asked, echoing the words she'd said to the girls earlier in the day. 'He'll stand by her.'

'Oh, of course he will. He'll be miserable forever. Jesus, people always said he took after his grandad, but now this is getting ridiculous.'

'What do you mean?'

'Oh, well, it was a pretty similar situation, I think. He met a girl, she got pregnant, and they had the baby, but it wasn't love. At least, I don't think it could have been. She only stuck around until the little one was one or two, then decided it wasn't what she wanted to do and left them both.'

Bex remembered Duncan mentioning it to her now, back when he had first been helping her in the study. Lorna was right. It really did feel like a case of history repeating itself. Not that she knew the ins and outs of the previous situation, but it seemed unlikely love could have been involved if the mother could walk away so early on in their baby's life.

'I can't imagine how tough that must have been, for his grandfather or his mother.'

'Right?' Lorna agreed. 'Duncan's ma didn't ever talk about it that much, but why would she? No one would ever want to talk about the fact that their mother walked out on them. I mean, dads – people sometimes get that, which is totally freaking wrong, because you know, 50 per cent DNA, but whatever. Still, the whole thing was a massive scandal, and they hadn't got married either. I think that's why Fergus let them stay in the house all this time. He hates stuff like scandal – wanted to shelter them from it.'

There was no denying Duncan's family didn't seem to have a lot of luck when it came to relationships. But the story sparked a different thought in Bex's mind. If the woman Duncan's grandad had got pregnant was someone he had only just met, then that couldn't be the woman in the photograph, could it? So maybe that was the one Fergus mentioned falling in love with. The one who had died before he got a chance to propose to her. And if her theory about them falling in love with the same person had been correct, then maybe Duncan's grandfather had only had a baby with his grandmother to try to push the loss of his true love out of his mind?

'Well, so what's your plan now?' Lorna asked, interrupting Bex's stream of romantic hypothesising. 'Avoid my brother, I take it?'

'Yeah. I think I'm going to stay a couple more days, get some bits sorted and then head back to London and work there for a bit.'

'I thought you were here for months?'

'I was, and I'll have to come back, but I could just do with a bit of a break from it.'

Lorna let out a long sigh. 'I know we haven't spent that much time together yet, but we'll still miss you. You haven't even come along to one of our Stitch and Bitch nights yet.'

'Stitch and Bitch nights?'

'Yeah... although Eilidh's the only one who really stitches. I just do the "bitch" part, and mostly about Katty. We're having one next Tuesday, and I really wanted you to come.'

'Maybe schedule one for when I'm back next time?'

'Okay, I can do that.' Lorna flashed her another smile. She was one of those people who just resonated warmth, and she wasn't alone in wishing they could have spent a bit more time together. Yet before Bex could say as much, Lorna was on her feet. 'Now, I guess I should put your food order into the kitchen, shouldn't I?' she said. 'You must be starving. And don't worry about paying. This one is going on my brother's tab. It's the least he owes you.'

51

Two hours later, Bex was opening the door to the castle, her stomach full, but the feeling of heaviness was coming from far more than just the weight of food. Even though it was now late afternoon and Fergus had given her the day off, she wanted to head into the study and sort through a few more things. See if it really was possible to get things packed away so she could work at home for at least a couple of weeks.

During the walk back, Duncan had tried to call her several times, but each time she had sent him to voicemail. Whatever he wanted to say to her, it wasn't going to make things easier. A clean break, the way she was trying to do, would be best in the long run, yet as she stepped inside the hallway to the castle, a surge of adrenaline swept through her. Fergus was talking to someone. Was it Duncan? And if it was, what the hell was she going to say to him? She could hardly tell him to leave when he had as much right to be there as she did.

She strained to hear who the laird was talking to, only to realise that it was only Fergus's voice she could hear. He was on the phone.

As she walked into the hallway, she saw him still standing there, with his mobile pressed against his ear. She couldn't help but feel surprised. She'd assumed he had a mobile phone, given how he'd mentioned ringing his sister a couple of times, but she'd never actually seen him use it. Unable to quench her sense of curiosity, she peered around into the drawing room to find Fergus standing with his hands on his hips, a deep scowl on his face.

'No, I've got to go. Aye, whatever. Aye, I hear you, lad. No. No. Yes, love to your ma too.' A moment later, he hung up and let out a long sigh. 'You might as well come in, rather than haverin' out there,' he said, raising his voice so Bex was in no doubt he was talking to her. Sheepishly, she slunk into the room.

'Everything all right?' she asked.

'Oh aye, just my nephew Kieron wanting another shoot here, sorting out dates in December. Why does it need sorting out now? He has free rein of the place; it's not like I'm holding any great balls or galas.'

'Would be nice, though,' Bex said absentmindedly. 'You know, a ball, when you've got all this space for it here.'

'Don't you start; you sound like him. And we have balls – we have Burns Night, and we have a ball at Christmas. Twice a year – that's plenty, as far as I'm concerned.'

A pang of sadness struck Bex. It would've been lovely to be here for one of those balls, she thought – to see everybody dressed up in their finery. To see Duncan dressed up in his kilt, a tartan that perfectly picked out the colour in his eyes. A shirt tight enough to outline the curve of his shoulder muscles and the strength of his back. She caught herself. *No, don't do that.* It was better this way. Better that she got going as soon as possible.

'Well, I was going to come looking for you anyway,' Fergus said. 'Young Duncan came around asking after you.'

'Did he?' Bex tried to sound neutral, but she felt her jaw clench.

'Aye, he left a note.'

'Oh.'

'The envelope was already open,' he added. 'I didn't read it.'

'I didn't think you did,' she said, holding it for a moment.

Fergus looked at her and raised his eyebrows, as if urging her to read. Bex wasn't sure why her hand was trembling. Why did it matter what Duncan had written? She could already imagine what would be on that piece of paper – apologies; long heartfelt words about needing to do the right thing; right person, wrong time, that sort of thing. That was what she expected.

But when she unfolded the note, she discovered it was far shorter than she'd anticipated.

Just two lines. Apparently, that was all he had to say to her.

Had to go away for a couple of days. Will explain when I get back. Sorry. Dx

52

Bex was furious. What kind of message was that? He was going away for a couple of days. No explanation. No mention of last night, or how he wished it could be different. Just the single word 'sorry', like that was enough to encapsulate all he needed to apologise for. Well, it wasn't.

Of course, it was the unwritten part of the note that angered her even more. By 'going away', he meant that he was going away with Katty, didn't he? Yes, of course he was going away with Katty. Somewhere they could be alone together. Discuss their future. He'd probably already apologised to her for Bex being at his house when she'd got there that morning. As if Katty was the one who needed the apology. He'd probably told her that it was a one-time thing and that there were no feelings involved. Purely physical. Meaningless. Those were the words he'd likely used, and the thought nauseated her. There wasn't a chance he'd tell her how he actually felt about Bex, not when it would only hurt her. Because Duncan didn't hurt people. Except her, that was. Yup, whether he'd wanted to or not, the truth was that he'd well and truly done a number on Bex.

If she needed any more confirmation that she had to get out of LochDarroch and back to London as soon as possible, this was it. She lifted her head and looked at Fergus.

'I'm going to head back to London,' she said. 'I can do some work from there for a week or so, but I could do with a hand packing up some of these ledgers. Any chance you could get Roddy or someone else to help me load them into the car?'

She was aware that she hadn't asked Fergus's permission for this, and that he would be well within his rights to question her decision from a work perspective. And understandably so. There was a good chance she would end up needing things she'd left behind, but she couldn't think about that. And thankfully, Fergus didn't. Instead, he nodded.

'Aye, I'll see who I can find,' he said. 'You go get your things together from your room. We'll sort this.'

As Bex shoved her clothes back into her suitcase, she was aware that she was being watched. 'It's not forever, girl,' she said, unable to meet the animal's eyes. 'But you knew this was going to happen. You have your life here. Your family's here. I don't. I was always going to have to leave.'

As she finally turned to face her, Ruby let out a long whine.

'I know, girl.' Bex sighed heavily as she dropped to the floor and buried her head in the dog's fur. 'I know exactly how you feel.'

Unfortunately, Roddy and Horace were both busy, so it was Fergus himself who helped Bex pack the ledgers and stacks of paper into the back of her car. Given the size of her suitcase, she couldn't fit nearly all of them, but it would be enough. She just needed a bit of a break – some space away from Duncan and away from the memories of him in the castle.

When the boot was full, she went to get another couple of boxes from the study to strap onto the back seat, but she had only just picked out which one she was going to take when there was a voice speaking from behind her.

'You have to be joking.'

Lorna stood in the doorway, and she hadn't come alone. She had Eilidh by her side as reinforcement.

'Did Fergus ring you?' Bex said. She didn't know whether to laugh or shout at the old man, but he clearly hadn't been as keen to let her go as he'd let on.

'You can't leave now,' Lorna said, ignoring Bex's question. 'You said you were going to go in a couple of days.'

'You don't want to make this decision when you're upset anyway,' Eilidh added. 'It's a long drive to make when your head's not straight.'

'I told you I needed space,' Bex said. 'I told you I was going to go early.'

'Yes, but not that early. Eilidh's right. You're not in the right frame of mind to go now. Please, let's just go for a drink first. Just so I know you're all right. Safe to drive.'

It was sweet how much they cared, but Bex shook her head. 'I can't have a drink. As you've already pointed out, I've got to drive back, and I need a clear head.'

'You can have a soft drink?'

She knew she wasn't going to get away with it, not without them seeing that she really was okay to drive. And this really was the best thing for her to do. She let out a long resigned sigh.

'Fine. I'll go for one lemonade – then I'm leaving.'

53

'I don't think he's going to stay with her, you know,' Eilidh said as they sat in the pub. They all had strong drinks, but just as Bex had said, she stuck to her lemonade.

She'd parked outside the pub, in a spot she was confident she'd be able to get out of quickly, although Lorna had ordered her a pint of the soft drink and it was clear they wanted to discuss the matter fully before they even thought about letting her go. And she'd understood that. Still, Bex's frustration had grown slightly when she'd had only a quarter of her drink left and Niall had appeared and immediately bought another round, including another pint of lemonade for Bex. At this rate, she was going to have to stop at every service station en route just for toilet breaks.

'Oh, he will,' Lorna said. 'He'll definitely take her back.'

'Honestly, no. I can't see that,' Eilidh insisted. 'She broke his heart. I don't think she will. And you didn't see him with... when... you know...' Eilidh's sentence drifted into nothing, but Bex knew exactly what she was struggling to say. Lorna hadn't seen him and her together. Eilidh had. Eilidh had seen them when Bex was doing a terrible job of pretending she wasn't interested in Duncan, and even then she'd seen straight through it. 'Besides, I never saw Katty as the maternal type,' Eilidh added, changing the direction of her comment so to divert attention away from Bex.

'Well, Duncan wants children,' Lorna said. 'Definitely. So maybe he'll raise it on his own.'

'And where does this leave Archie in all this mess? Does anyone know if Katty's even seen him?'

They were all talking around her, but Bex could barely listen. Instead, images kept floating through her mind – images of Katty and Duncan, sitting together at a doctor's appointment, holding each other's hands, tears in their eyes as they looked at the ultrasound of the baby together. Images of the wedding. She was sure it would go ahead now, too. Would they still have it at The Haven? At the place where they had shared their first kiss? The thought made bile sting at the back of her throat.

'Hey,' she said, breaking in, 'I really appreciate this, but I want to get down to Glasgow by tonight.'

'I'm not sure that's going to happen,' Niall said. He had been pretty quiet most of the evening, letting the girls talk while he kept his attention fixed on his phone, but now he glanced up at the group, looking decidedly pale. 'Sorry, Bex, but I think you're going to have to delay your leaving. The ford's flooded. None of the cars are getting through.'

'What?' Bex's jaw dropped as she shook her head in disbelief. 'It can't be.'

He turned his phone around and showed her a Facebook post of a road. One she recognised; it was the one she'd come in on. The ford that she'd walked through barefoot to ensure the car wouldn't get stuck. But that was exactly what had happened to someone. Their little yellow car was bobbing in the water, the stranded owner photographed still trapped inside.

'How?' she asked. 'It hasn't rained in days.'

'There's been some trouble with the lochs, I think,' Niall said. 'They're trying to sort out the dams or something. That must be what's done it.'

'Great,' she muttered. She didn't even know lochs had dams. 'I'll have to go the other way.'

'You mean the other way that adds three hours to your trip?' Eilidh said. 'That's just silly. You might as well stay until morning.'

'Hey, look at it this way,' Lorna said, nudging her. 'At least now we get to give you a proper farewell, right?'

Bex let out a groan, but Lorna grinned.

'You can stay at mine. We'll have an impromptu Stitch and Bitch night.'

'Without the sewing part, though,' Eilidh clarified with a smile. 'Obviously, without the sewing.'

'Well, yes,' Lorna said, before picking up Bex's lemonade and moving it to the edge of the table. 'Now that's decided, let's get you a proper drink. A double shot, I think. And I know exactly whose tab we're going to put it on. Again. Actually, I think the whole night's going to be on him.'

Bex wondered whether Lorna knew that it was Fergus who paid off Duncan's tabs at the pubs, rather than Duncan himself, but she wasn't going to disagree. Regardless of who was paying, she needed to drink.

54

Bex blinked once, only to scrunch her eyes tightly back together. The light was blinding, sending sharp pain from her temples all the way to the back of her throat. How many drinks had she had last night? She couldn't remember. After the news about the flooded ford, Lorna had swapped Bex's lemonade for something a lot stronger and brought out shots for them all to do in celebration of Bex staying an extra night. She remembered that. Just like she remembered Niall having a go at mixing cocktails behind the bar and insisting everyone try them. If Bex's memory served her right, that included old Moira, the ancient matriarch who sat like a gargoyle in the corner.

Either way, everything hurt, and her throat felt like she'd swallowed a porcupine.

With a loud groan that made the headache even worse, Bex rolled over, expecting the large expanse of her double bed to stretch out onto, only to hit the hard floor with a thud.

'Argh!' She squeezed her eyes shut against the pain, which, after the impact, was no longer contained to every inch of her skull. As she lay there, unsure which part of her body she could try to clutch, thundering footsteps rattled through the floor-boards, rushing towards her.

'Bex, are you all right? What happened?' She opened her eyes to see Lorna's face peering down at her. 'Did you fall off the sofa?'

'Did I sleep here?' Bex asked, her voice croaking into life. With a light chuckle, Lorna offered her hand and helped pull her up.

'You didn't want to go back to the castle, so you crashed on the sofa. But clearly forgot. Didn't I tell you it was a sofa bed? You could have pulled it out to make it bigger.'

Given that Bex had no recollection of getting here last night, imagining that she would have been able to work out the mechanics of an unknown sofa bed in her previously inebriated state felt very optimistic, even for Lorna.

'How much did we drink?' she asked as she sat herself up.

'Quite a lot.'

'How are you feeling?'

'Awful,' Lorna said, though Bex found that hard to believe. She was upright to start with. And she seemed to be speaking without sending spasms of pain shooting through her skull. That was better than Bex on both levels.

'Oh God,' Bex said when she saw the way light was rolling in beneath the curtains. 'I wanted to get going early.'

'There's no way you're going anywhere now. Come on, let's go to the café. We'll get lunch. You're probably still three times over the limit to drive.'

'Lunch? What time is it?'

'Nearly noon.'

Bex let out a groan. She was now almost a day behind her plan to get out. But Lorna was right. There was no chance she could drive in this state. At the very least she needed a cold shower and several strong shots of caffeine. Although just the thought of the word 'shot' caused nausea to billow through her.

'I'm not sure I'm going to be able to eat anything,' she said.

'Sure you will. Come on. We'll start with some dry toast and work up from there.'

Realising there was no world in which Lorna took no for an answer, and thinking that perhaps agreeing to go with her was the one way to stop her from talking so loudly, Bex dragged herself up onto her feet.

'Fine,' she said. 'But after breakfast, I'm leaving.'

She should have realised a café wouldn't be a great place for someone whose head felt like there was a herd of rhinos tap-dancing behind their temples, and so, as they walked in, Bex headed to the table in the corner and dropped her head down between her elbows, trying to ignore the smell of coffee that pervaded her senses.

Normally she wouldn't have any issues with coffee when she was hungover. Often, it was the one thing that genuinely helped. Only now the scent reminded her of the coffee gift Duncan had given her. Thoughts of Duncan inevitably brought an uncomfortable squirm in her stomach that made her nausea even worse. But Lorna insisted she eat something.

'Well, that was an unexpectedly heavy night,' Lorna said when she came back from ordering their food. 'It's a good job I'm not working. There'd be no chance of anyone getting the right orders today.'

'Is it worrying that my memories are so fuzzy from last night?' Bex asked, clutching her head. 'I can remember singing though. Lots of singing. Were we singing?'

'We?' Lorna put full emphasis on the word. 'No, there was no *we* about it. You were singing, Bex. Apparently, you like karaoke.'

'Oh God. Was it bad?'

'Well, you can see the video for yourself if you want...' Lorna moved to pick up her phone, but Bex's hand shot out in front of her.

'No, no, don't!' Bex said, pushing Lorna's phone away. 'I don't want to see. I don't want to know.'

'Don't worry, you didn't do anything stupid,' Lorna assured her. 'Well, not that stupid anyway. The singing was probably the worst of it.'

Probably. That was the word in the sentence that Bex didn't like.

'I didn't, you know, ring Duncan or anything, did I?'

'No.' Lorna shook her head, laughing. 'You had no intention of ringing him at all. In fact, you yelled at anyone if they even mentioned his name. It was, in your words' – she lifted her hands to do air quotes – '"a Duncan-Free Zone".'

Bex let out a long sigh. She knew all too well that drunk phone calls were never a sensible idea, but part of her still craved to hear from him. To demand more of an apology than the scant note he had written her.

Rather than just the plain toast Bex had asked for, Lorna had ordered them both full Scottish breakfasts and just the sight of it was enough to turn Bex's stomach. Still, she took her time, cutting off tiny mouthfuls and chewing excessively slowly. Though after forty minutes, when the beans were stone cold, the eggs congealed and the tattie scones soggy, she could manage no more.

'I guess I should get going,' she said. 'I need to start the drive, get as far as I can.'

'And I'm guessing nothing I can say will persuade you otherwise?' Lorna said, her eyes pleading.

Bex shook her head. 'No, sorry.'

'Fine, then let me walk you to your car.'

As they stepped out onto the road, the loud sound of bleating rattled through her. Bex had grown used to the sound of sheep since moving here, on her walks around the loch and castle grounds that woke her each morning. But this sounded particularly loud. She assumed it was another side effect of her extreme hangover – that was, until Lorna spoke.

'I think you might have to delay your plans to leave for a little while longer,' she said, nodding towards the road ahead.

Bex looked up, eyes widening. A huge flock of sheep had gathered across the road, blocking the exit entirely.

55

'Who do they belong to? Where have they all come from?' Bex asked, staring at the droves of sheep. There had to be two hundred of them, and they were blocking the entire road. The cacophony of bleating was worse than being in the middle of a rock concert, and the way the animals seemed determined to stay fixed on the spot and not let anyone else past was irritatingly similar to some of the gigs she had been to too.

'Surely this can't be allowed. People have to be able to get somewhere.'

'I guess they're moving fields,' Lorna said. 'Not sure whose they are. Maybe Fergus's?'

'Well, they need to move them faster.'

Lorna laughed. 'Said like a true city girl. I know it's annoying, but maybe you could do a bit more work up at the castle for a couple of hours. Or if not, just consider it an extra day on holiday. This is a holiday spot, you know – you could go down to the loch or—'

'I don't want to go down to the loch. I want to get away from here, that's all,' Bex snapped before catching herself, her hand

going to her head as she shook it in apology. 'I'm sorry. I'm just...
I haven't done any work for a day and a half and on top of everything else, falling behind is the last thing I need.'

'Then why don't you look at today as an early weekend,'
Lorna suggested, 'and do your work on Saturday and Sunday?
You can do that, right? People do that in jobs all the time, don't
they?'

'Possibly.'

As much as Bex loved Lorna's free-and-easy approach to
things, that wasn't what had gotten Bex where she was in her
job. The truth was, she had told Nigel earlier in the week just
how massive the task was, and his response had been not to
worry about it, so she didn't have a hard deadline. But the
longer she stayed, the greater the chance of Duncan returning
before she left, and that was what she wanted to avoid. It wasn't
really about work or traffic – she just didn't want to see
Duncan.

'I know you're under a lot of stress, but these things have a
way of working out,' Lorna said, trying to be helpful. 'And even if
they don't, sweating won't make it any better.'

She was right. Bex knew that. But that still didn't mean it was
easy. Telling someone not to stress was a little like telling them
not to think about a pink elephant; all it did was remind you
how much you had to worry about.

'Actually,' Bex said, eyeing the flock in front of her, 'the sheep
are moving faster than I thought. I reckon they'll be gone in an
hour, so I can leave then and just get to Glasgow a bit later.'

'You sure you want to do that?' Lorna said. 'You still had a
pretty late night last night. You must be fairly shattered. I know
I am.'

'It's fine. It's not like it's winter or anything – I don't mind
driving late as long as it's light.'

'Right, of course. So, what do you want to do until then? Café? My place? Or back to the castle?'

Bex thought about it. The castle was definitely out. That was the one thing she knew for certain, and she wasn't sure she wanted to sit around food any longer. Also, while the throbbing behind her temples had eased, it was still definitely there.

'Would it be really wrong of me if I just had a nap at yours?' she asked.

Lorna smiled. 'Of course not. That's what friends are for, and this time, I'll even pull the sofa bed out for you, too.'

56

When they got back to Lorna's, she reached down the side of the sofa and pulled on a small handle. Immediately, the entire front section pulled out and converted the piece of furniture into a full-size bed.

'Why the hell didn't we do that last night?' Bex said, still feeling the bruise down her arm from where she'd rolled off the sofa just a few hours before.

'Well, I'm sure I told you about it at some point, but we were probably too drunk to remember,' Lorna said, laughing. 'But I got you a blanket and pillow, didn't I? Considering the state I was in, I think that was pretty good going.'

Bex dropped onto the sofa bed, her muscles sinking into the soft springs. Yes, coming for a nap was definitely the right choice to make. She grabbed the pillow and blanket Lorna had fetched for her, kicked off her shoes and lay back.

'Thanks,' Bex said, navigating the alarm app on her phone. 'I'll just set this for an hour – that should be enough for a decent nap before I head home.'

'Sounds good. I'm going to head out to meet Eilidh for a bit. You don't mind being on your own, do you?'

The fact that Lorna was still able to walk and talk coherently was all the evidence Bex needed that she wasn't suffering nearly as much, but then she was three or four years younger. Maybe it made all the difference. Or maybe she was just more used to whatever the hell they'd been drinking than she was.

'No, of course not,' Bex replied. 'If you're not back by the time I go... well, thank you for everything. You've really made my time here enjoyable. And you know I'll be back soon, but maybe if you fancy a trip down south you can come and visit me in London? I'll take you to Wildflower Lock. I think you'd really like it there.'

'That sounds great,' Lorna said. 'I'd like that. A big road trip and everything.' She hovered for a moment as if there was more she wanted to say. And there probably was. Something about Duncan and how sorry she was at how it had all ended up. That was what Bex wanted to say, anyway. But she didn't.

No more words were spoken. Instead, they exchanged a warm hug, after which Bex offered Lorna a last wave as she disappeared out of the door. As she let out a heavy sigh, Bex collapsed back onto the sofa bed. Her eyes barely closed before she was fast asleep.

* * *

The alarm blasted through her skull, jerking her awake. Bex felt as if she had barely closed her eyes, and yet the hour had passed.

'Lorna?' she called into the flat. No response. Bex wasn't surprised; she didn't know her new friend well, but she could tell Lorna wasn't the type for a quick catch-up. No doubt she was probably out with Eilidh gossiping about last night. A memory stirred in the back of Bex's mind. She might have got it wrong, but she had a vague recollection of Niall confessing his love to Eilidh, or maybe the others had just been egging him on to do it. She wasn't sure. Either way, she was relieved Lorna wasn't there; she'd already done her goodbyes and didn't want to have to go through it again.

Ready to finally say goodbye to LochDarroch – at least for a little while – she headed out the front door and closed it behind her. Just as she'd hoped, the sheep were gone. She could still hear a faint bleating in the distance, but at least her car was where she'd parked it, by the side of the road, with no animals in sight. It looked like she could finally leave.

But as she approached her vehicle, something caught her attention. Her trusty coupé was at an odd angle, as though it were sloped. Had she parked it like that, with one of the front wheels up? She couldn't remember – it felt like ages ago now and to be fair, she had been so upset, she could have parked it in the flooded ford and barely noticed. Though as she got closer, her heart sank.

It wasn't that the ground was sloped, or the front wheel that was raised at all. No, the reason for the peculiar angle of her car was very obvious: her back tyre was flat.

Bex's jaw clicked as her back molars ground together.

'You have got to be kidding me.'

57

The anger was rising within her. Seriously? Would the world just not cut her a break?

There, on the ground, next to the bottom of the tyre, was the tyre cap. By the looks of things, it had been knocked off, but how? Sheep. That was the immediate answer that came into her head. The flock of sheep earlier in the day would likely be the reason for that, wouldn't it? As Bex contemplated the scenarios, questions rose in her mind. Like, how would they manage to do that? It was a screw cap. The only way they would have been able to knock it off was if it had been loose in the first place, and even then, didn't the valves have some sort of safety to mean that the air couldn't just pour out?

Well, air had definitely poured out of her tyre. The bottom section was totally horizontal, with the rim of the rubber slumping outwards.

'Everything okay?'

Bex turned around to find Roddy standing behind her, concern etched on his face.

'Not really,' she said. Tears were brimming in her eyes, but she refused to let them fall. 'Honestly, I just wanted to get out of this place and it's been one thing after another. What with the flood, and the sheep, and now this.'

'What flood?' Roddy asked.

'The ford,' she told him. 'The one a couple of miles outside of the village. It was flooded last night when I wanted to leave. Apparently, it was something to do with one of the dams on the loch.'

'Are you sure?'

'Yes, I'm sure,' Bex said, trying not to sound sharp. 'I was ready to leave, to head back to London, but Niall showed me the photos.'

The frown that had been on Roddy's face since they started their conversation was still there, only now it was getting deeper.

'What time was this?' he said. 'I came through it about five and everything was bonnie then.'

'It was a bit later than that. Around seven.'

'And it was definitely that ford?'

'Yes. It was.' Bex knew how exasperated she sounded, but really, after the previous thirty-six hours, the last thing she needed was to go in circles with a conversation that was leading nowhere. If Roddy would help her with her flat tyre, then great, but if not, this conversation was just more wasted time. Still, he didn't let the point lie.

'But it's summer. The only time I've ever known that to happen was when there was daft rainfall,' he said.

Bex was grinding her teeth again. She was going to have to tell Roddy to stop talking, or at least ask him about the tyre, but he was still prattling on about the bloody flooded ford.

'Last time was this spring just gone,' he mused. 'In April. Then it was really flooded. This poor woman got her wee yellow car stuck in the middle of it and everything—'

'Sorry, Roddy, but could you—' Bex cut herself short. 'I'm sorry. Did you say it was a yellow car that got stuck?'

'Yeah, one of those wee things. Three doors. No room to swing a cat. Probably better in a city than somewhere like here, but—'

'Do you have a photo?' Bex asked. Her pulse was rising, as if it was trying to tell her this was more than just a coincidence.

'Sorry?' Roddy said.

'A photo of the car,' she repeated. 'Do you have one?'

His nose scrunched a little.

'I could probably find one online. One sec.'

A minute later, after several taps and sweeps on his screen, Roddy handed Bex his phone to look at. Every muscle in her jaw tensed.

'Lorna,' she growled before picking up her phone.

58

'I know what you've done,' Bex said as soon as Lorna picked up the phone.

'Bex, are you still here?' Lorna's voice had a cheery tone, yet Bex heard the nervousness rolling behind her words.

'Yes, I'm still here. Even though I could have left last night because the ford wasn't flooded at all. Did you do the tyre too? You know that's vandalism.'

'So you are still here?'

It was a good job they were having a telephone call, because if they had been talking face to face, Bex was pretty sure she would be ringing her neck.

'I'll take it from your lack of response that you are the reason my back tyre is flat? Just like you're the reason Niall told me that the road was flooded so that I couldn't get out? Did you arrange the sheep too, so my car couldn't get out the village?'

'Of course I didn't. That was pure luck. Incredibly well timed, I have to say.'

Bex let out a wail of annoyance.

'Oh my God, Lorna – why would you not just let me leave? You're supposed to be my friend.'

'I am your friend, I absolutely am,' Lorna said, her voice sounding choked. 'Which is exactly why I couldn't let you leave until you'd spoken to Duncan. I'm sorry, it was wrong of me, but please... I spoke to him last night, just before I let the air out of your tyre and I promised I wouldn't say anything to you, but I know he's going to be back soon, and I know you two are perfect for each other. You've just got to talk this through, please.'

Bex was seething. She had heard all about village mentality and the way people living in small communities like this would feel they had the right to stick their noses into everyone else's business, even when they definitely didn't. But she was not a village person, and she was less than impressed with being manipulated. Especially by someone who had proclaimed to be her friend.

'Let me make this perfectly clear,' Bex said, aware that her voice was raised a good few decibels above what was considered polite. 'I don't want to speak to Duncan. I have nothing to say to him. Whatever happened between us was obviously one colossal mistake, as has been proven by everything that's happened since. Duncan and I are nothing. We will never be anything and my life would be perfectly okay if I never have to set eyes on Duncan again.'

'That's a shame.'

The sound of the voice behind her was enough to make her stomach flip and her heart somersault, and in that instant, as the air quivered in her lungs, she knew that everything she had just said to Lorna was untrue. She had wanted to see Duncan again, so much it made her body ache. That was why she didn't look up the ford herself, or ask anyone else at the pub about it. That was why she had drunk so much the night before, so that she could block the image of him with his hands touching her out of her mind. She wanted to hold him and kiss him and never let anything get between them.

But that couldn't happen now, could it?

She hadn't thought so, and yet as her legs trembled and she turned slowly around, she knew exactly who she was going to find there.

'Hey, Barker. I heard you were planning on leaving,' he said. 'And I'm not sure I can let you do that.'

59

He looked like he hadn't slept in days. There were bags under his eyes, and his cheeks were sunken in, and yet it was his gaze that held her completely. Those blue-green eyes that she had first laid eyes on all those weeks ago in her bathroom. Only they hadn't looked at her then like they were looking at her now.

'I thought you were away for a couple of days,' she said, her voice cracking as she hung up the phone to Lorna without so much as a goodbye.

'That was the plan,' he said, 'but I had several emergency phone calls saying I had to get back to the village immediately.'

Bex scoffed. 'Let me guess, Lorna?'

'Lorna and the old man, too.'

'Fergus?'

He nodded. 'He was worried that I'd driven off his new accountant. And it's tough to get good hires out here.'

He flashed her a smile. The type that would normally make her insides melt, only she held firm, steeling herself against the tides of emotion that were rolling through her. She wasn't going to let that happen. She needed to leave now, with whatever shreds of heart remained intact.

'Katty's pregnant,' she whispered.

'Yes, she is,' Duncan said slowly. 'But it's not mine. It's Archie's.'

'What?'

He let out a sad chuckle, the sound barely raised before it faded into nothing, leaving him looking even worse than he had before. Bex was hit with a sudden urge to run across to him, to wrap her arms around him and say that everything would be okay, but she didn't. She stood there.

'Then why did she come to you?'

Her feet were rooted to the ground, but Duncan seemed to be getting closer to her. He was the one moving towards her, she realised. Closing the gap between them.

'Archie freaked out,' he said. 'Suddenly started feeling guilty about everything. She wanted me to talk to him. That was why she came to the lodge. It was never about us, and even if it had been, even if she had come to beg for another chance...' He paused and lifted his hand, cupping Bex's cheek in his palm. Her eyes involuntarily closed at the warmth that felt so familiar. So secure. 'It wouldn't have mattered what she wanted. I'm not hers any more. I'm not hers, Barker. I'm yours. One hundred per cent.'

Duncan shifted his thumb to wipe a stray tear from her cheek. A stray tear she hadn't even realised had fallen.

'But the note? Why didn't you tell me that?'

'I'm sorry,' he said, edging back a little as he looked her in the eye. 'I wasn't trying to be cryptic. I just saw you hadn't read my messages or answered my calls, and I just scribbled it down. All I was thinking about was getting the visit to Archie over and done with as quickly as possible so that I could get back to you.

But in hindsight, maybe that's what I should have put in the note.'

'You think?' Bex let out a dry chuckle, causing yet more tears to tumble free.

'I'm sorry,' he said. 'Look, I meant what I said about taking one day at a time, but that's up to you. I'm all in here. And I promise, I will never do anything to hurt you. I swear, on Kenna's life.'

Bex chuckled again. But this time, there were no tears. Just a fluttering in her chest. 'Well, vows don't get any bigger than that,' she said.

'You're right. They don't.'

He was so close, she could smell that sweet aroma of pine rising from his body. Feel the warmth of his breath and the rising of anticipation tingling in her chest.

'I think this is the moment I ask if I can kiss you again,' he whispered in her ear.

'I don't think you have to ask any more,' Bex said. 'I think you can pretty much assume that the answer's going to be yes from now on.'

'Thank goodness for that.' He leaned forward, his eyes still on hers as their lips met.

The moment they connected, the cheers erupted. Bex broke away from Duncan to look behind her to see not only Lorna but also Roddy and Niall there, clapping and wolf-whistling, but Bex's eyes moved past them to a figure standing a little way back. An old man, in a muddy wax jacket and flat cap, with a horde of dogs sitting around him. When Bex met his gaze, he smiled slightly before dipping his chin in a nod.

'Don't tell me you were in on this too?' she said, finally releasing her hands from Duncan to walk across to Fergus.

'I have no idea what you're on about,' he said. 'I was just here walking the dogs. That's all.'

'Is that right?' she said.

A twinkle shone out in the old man's eyes and before Bex could stop herself, she leaned forwards and hugged him tightly. When she broke away, she could have sworn there was a slight sheen to his eyes. Though before she could be sure, he lowered his head, and by the time he raised it again, both the sheen and the smile were gone, replaced with a deep scowl.

'Well, if we're done with all the havering, can you get back to the castle and carry on with work, please?' he said. 'Those accounts winnae sort themselves.'

Bex turned back to Duncan, whose grin was so wide it made her heart throb.

'You heard the old man,' he said. 'Let's go home.'

EPILOGUE

'I'm gonna be like a fifth wheel now on dates,' Lorna whinged as they met at the pub the following week.

'What are you on about?' Eilidh said. 'Niall and I are still single, right?'

Lorna rolled her eyes and threw a glance at Bex, who couldn't help but chuckle.

Obviously, Bex had had to forgive Lorna for all the pranks she had pulled to keep her there, though Duncan had assured her that he would have driven down to London to get her back if that's what it had taken, and she had believed him.

'So, how long until you need to go back to London?' Lorna said. 'I heard you've still got a ton to go.'

'I reckon about another two months,' she said. 'But we'll work something out,' she added, glancing across at Duncan. Her hand was in his, as it had been most of the time since he had come back from seeing Archie. Every spare minute they spent together, and even those that weren't spare, when Bex had ended up working slightly later some evenings, or Duncan had needed to do something on the grounds on the weekend, the other had been there at their side, doing what they could to help.

'Well, we better get back,' Bex said, standing up. 'We need to go spend some time with Kenna. She's been cross about all the nights Duncan spent up at the castle.'

'But Ruby gets upset if Bex is at the lodge too much,' Duncan countered, slipping his arm around her waist. 'Don't drink too much,' he said with a glance to his sister. 'We'll see you later in the week.'

'You better,' Lorna said, blowing them both a kiss farewell.

They kept a slow pace back towards the lodge, occasionally stopping to watch a rabbit nibbling on the grass, or a hawk hovering above them, or sometimes just to kiss. Bex didn't always find it easy, knowing that at some point this time together would come to an end and Bex would have to go back to London. But she tried not to dwell on it. This, here with Duncan, was the happiest she could remember being in any relationship ever, and she wasn't going to let an unknown future ruin that for them.

As they reached the lodge, Duncan opened the door, only to take one step inside and stop.

'Seriously, girl?' he said, letting out a groan. 'We were away for one night. That was it.'

It only took Bex a moment to see what he was talking about. She hadn't been joking about Kenna getting cross when they didn't stay at the lodge, and when Kenna was cross, you knew it.

This time, she had knocked several picture frames off the shelves, along with half a dozen books and one hefty-looking photo album. All lay scattered on the floor.

'You sort that side of the room, I'll do this one,' Bex said to Duncan. Moving over to the photo album, she lifted it up, ready to pop it back on the shelf, only to stop and stare at the open page.

'Wow,' she said. 'Is this you?' It was a picture of a small boy on a tricycle. From the cheeky grin on his face, she was fairly certain it was Duncan she was looking at.

'Yeah, little me.'

'You were super cute.'

'And still super cute,' he said, coming up behind her and wrapping his arms around her waist. 'Aye, these are some of the only photos I've got from when I was a kid. The only ones I've got with me and Mum. There's one of her just here, I think. Aye, look, there she is.'

He turned to the next page. Little Duncan was still wearing his cycling helmet, though he was no longer on the bike, but rather than studying him, Bex's eyes were drawn to the woman.

There was something about her. The curve of her eyebrows, the softness of her chin – she looked unbelievably familiar, but she couldn't place why. Was it just because of the similarities to Duncan? Maybe, but then why did she feel like she'd seen another photo of her somewhere?

'Do you have photos of your mum up?' she said, glancing around the room to work out if that was why she recognised her so much. But Duncan shook his head.

'No. I did, but then someone broke a frame with her in and it tore the photo.' He shot a glance at Kenna, who was busy licking her paws without a care in the world. 'I keep meaning to hang some up on the walls. Why?'

Why? That question rolled around her head. She could hardly say because she thought she recognised her. Not when she had no idea why that would be. She was just tired, that was all.

'No reason.' She closed the photo album and placed it back

on the shelf before turning around and looping her arms around Duncan's neck. 'Now, remind me, wasn't there something we were planning on doing tonight?'

A coy smile flickered on his lips.

He leaned towards her, his smile a mirror image of her own.

'Aye, I think you're right. Now why don't you remind me what that was...'

* * *

MORE FROM HANNAH LYNN

Another book from Hannah Lynn, *In at the Deep End*, is available to order now here:

www.mybook.to/InDeepEnd

ACKNOWLEDGEMENTS

I do hope you enjoyed reading this story as much as I enjoyed writing it. The moment I finished Wildflower Lock, I knew it was time for Bex to step out of her role as best friend and become the leading lady and I am so grateful to you, my readers, for coming on the journey with her. And don't worry, that journey's not over yet.

As always, my biggest thanks go to my readers, without whom I would not be here, and also my family. In particular my husband, Jake, who works tirelessly behind the scenes, making this wonderful life of mine possible.

Thank you to Emily my editor and the team who helped the book come to life.

ABOUT THE AUTHOR

Hannah Lynn is the author of over twenty books spanning several genres. Hannah grew up in the Cotswolds, UK. After graduating from university, she spent 15 years as a teacher of physics, teaching in the UK, Thailand, Malaysia, Austria and Jordan.

Sign up to Hannah Lynn's mailing list here for news, competitions and updates on future books.

Visit Hannah's website: www.hannahlynnauthor.com

Follow Hannah on social media:

facebook.com/hannahlynnauthor
instagram.com/hannahlynnwrites
bookbub.com/authors/hannah-lynn

Boldwood

Boldwood Books is an award-winning fiction publishing company seeking out the best stories from around the world.

Find out more at www.boldwoodbooks.com

Join our reader community for brilliant books, competitions and offers!

Follow us

@BoldwoodBooks

@TheBoldBookClub

Printed in Dunstable, United Kingdom